LOVE AT THE TOWER

They both laughed and Robina caught something in his eyes that told her he had more to say.

"But that is not the reason I have asked you here," the Earl added.

Robina stayed silent, although inside her thoughts were far from still.

She felt nervous and uneasy.

"Robina," the Earl continued slowly, enfolding her hands with his hands. "I have been thinking of nothing but you for these past few days and I must tell you that I am utterly in love with you.

"That appalling business with Ellis has only served to compound what I was already feeling. If I am honest, I have loved you since we were children together and I am not a man to hold back when I have made my mind up, so I would be honoured if you will agree to be my wife."

Robina stood there with the wind blowing through her hair and the Earl holding onto her hands.

She looked into eyes that were so full of love that she could scarcely meet his gaze and did not know how to answer him.

"Please, Robina, what do you say to me?" he asked, pleadingly, his blue eyes willing her to open up her heart to him.

A heart that at that very moment was wracked with confusion and astonishment.

THE BARBARA CARTLAND PINK COLLECTION

Titles in this series

LOVE AT THE TOWER

BARBARA CARTLAND

Barbaracartland.com Ltd

THE BARBARA CARTLAND PINK COLLECTION

Barbara Cartland was the most prolific bestselling author in the history of the world. She was frequently in the Guinness Book of Records for writing more books in a year than any other living author. In fact her most amazing literary feat was when her publishers asked for more Barbara Cartland romances, she doubled her output from 10 books a year to over 20 books a year, when she was 77.

She went on writing continuously at this rate for 20 years and wrote her last book at the age of 97, thus completing 400 books between the ages of 77 and 97.

Her publishers finally could not keep up with this phenomenal output, so at her death she left 160 unpublished manuscripts, something again that no other author has ever achieved.

Now the exciting news is that these 160 original unpublished Barbara Cartland books are already being published and by Barbaracartland.com exclusively on the internet, as the international web is the best possible way of reaching so many Barbara Cartland readers around the world.

The 160 books are published monthly and will be numbered in sequence.

The series is called the Pink Collection as a tribute to Barbara Cartland whose favourite colour was pink and it became very much her trademark over the years.

The Barbara Cartland Pink Collection is published only on the internet. Log on to www.barbaracartland.com to find out how you can purchase the books monthly as they are published, and take out a subscription that will ensure that all subsequent editions are delivered to you by mail order to your home.

NEW

Barbaracartland.com is proud to announce the publication of ten new Audio Books for the first time as CDs. They are favourite Barbara Cartland stories read by well-known actors and actresses and each story extends to 4 or 5 CDs. The Audio Books are as follows:

The Patient Bridegroom	The Passion and the Flower
A Challenge of Hearts	Little White Doves of Love
A Train to Love	The Prince and the Pekinese
The Unbroken Dream	A King in Love
The Cruel Count	A Sign of Love

More Audio Books will be published in the future and the above titles can be purchased by logging on to the website www.barbaracartland.com or please write to the address below.

If you do not have access to a computer, you can write for information about the Barbara Cartland Pink Collection and the Barbara Cartland Audio Books to the following address:

Barbara Cartland.com Ltd., Camfield Place,
Hatfield, Hertfordshire AL9 6JE, United Kingdom.

Telephone: +44 (0)1707 642629
Fax: +44 (0)1707 663041

THE LATE DAME BARBARA CARTLAND

Barbara Cartland who sadly died in May 2000 at the age of nearly 99 was the world's most famous romantic novelist who wrote 723 books in her lifetime with worldwide sales of over 1 billion copies and her books were translated into 36 different languages.

As well as romantic novels, she wrote historical biographies, 6 autobiographies, theatrical plays, books of advice on life, love, vitamins and cookery. She also found time to be a political speaker and television and radio personality.

She wrote her first book at the age of 21 and this was called *Jigsaw*. It became an immediate bestseller and sold 100,000 copies in hardback and was translated into 6 different languages. She wrote continuously throughout her life, writing bestsellers for an astonishing 76 years. Her books have always been immensely popular in the United States, where in 1976 her current books were at numbers 1 & 2 in the B. Dalton bestsellers list, a feat never achieved before or since by any author.

Barbara Cartland became a legend in her own lifetime and will be best remembered for her wonderful romantic novels, so loved by her millions of readers throughout the world.

Her books will always be treasured for their moral message, her pure and innocent heroines, her good looking and dashing heroes and above all her belief that the power of love is more important than anything else in everyone's life.

"Love is the same for everybody – it is sublime, ethereal and heavenly – whether you live in a castle or a cottage."

Barbara Cartland

CHAPTER ONE
1897

Robina Melville stared out of the carriage window and sighed. The sun was setting over the green countryside as she sped towards her Surrey home in Lucksham.

Seated beside her was Nanny – an elderly lady who had brought up her mother as well as Robina.

But Robina's mother was no longer with her. She had died the previous year and so distraught was her father that he had sent Robina to stay with friends in France.

"It is for the best, Robina, my dear," he had said to her on the day he had called her into the library at the rear of the huge rambling building that was Trentham House.

How she had shed copious tears as he had sat there at his desk, almost impassively telling her that he wished to be alone and that he had written to his friends in Paris, the Lamonts, asking them to take Robina in as a guest.

"But I don't want to go to France – my place is here with you," she had protested with even more tears running down her lovely face.

At the age of twenty-one, she had known so much sorrow, far too much for one so young.

Her beloved Mama's long illness had taken its toll on everyone concerned.

At first the doctors had said it was merely a chill on her stomach that had made her double up in agony one day playing tennis, but then a swelling in her stomach grew and it became apparent that this was not a chill at all.

Robina's father had sent for a specialist doctor from Switzerland and for a short time her mother had seemed to rally round and improve.

But despite massive doctor's bills and a medicine chest that groaned with pills and potions, herb tinctures and poultices, she got worse.

Robina could recall the day that she collapsed and retired to bed, never to get up again.

It had been a fine June afternoon and a garden party was being held in the gardens of Trentham House.

"You must put on your best dress today," Nanny had said to her, "your Mama will surely want you to look as attractive as possible for her guests."

Robina admired the white lawn dress with lovely Nottingham lace on the bodice and cuffs. She had travelled all the way up to London to have it made at her Mama's dressmakers.

Pulling on the gown, she wondered what cook had in store for them. She was famous throughout the County for her cakes and pastries.

"Do you think that there will be any young people of my own age present?" she had asked Nanny, as she put Robina's hair up into an elegant French knot and carefully pinned her new summer hat on top.

"I would think so, dear. After all it is a very special occasion."

"I hope that Mama is much better today as she did look terribly pale at dinner last night."

"She will be as right as rain, Robina – you must not worry so about her. This doctor from Switzerland seems to have worked miracles with her."

2

"But she hardly ate anything over dinner – " sighed Robina, admiring her reflection in the mirror.

"Your Mama has never had a large appetite, which is why she still boasts the same slender waist she had as a girl. Now, come along, Robina, your Mama and Papa will want you downstairs to greet their guests as they arrive."

Robina ran downstairs and saw that their footman was already showing people into the garden.

Walking past a rose-covered arch, she noticed that her mother was chatting to a large group of people.

'How pale she looks,' she thought to herself.

As she approached her mother turned and smiled.

"Darling, do come and join us – Lord Hampton was just telling us about his son Robert's exploits in India."

The old man's face lit up as Robina walked across the lawn towards them.

"Robina, my dear, how lovely you look," he said, and almost immediately, began to cough.

Lady Melville signalled to Newman to bring a glass of water. The Earl was bright red in the face as he gulped it down.

"You will have to excuse me, my dear, but I fear I am not as well as I could be. Those blasted doctors know nothing and cannot help me!"

Robina looked on in dismay as he was struggling to compose himself.

She had known the Earl since childhood and as a girl had played with his sons, Robert and Ellis.

Robert was the elder of the two brothers and was in India with his Regiment – she had not seen him for ages – not since he was sent away to Eton in fact.

He had then gone to the Royal Military College at

Sandhurst and from there, had been sent on a Commission to India.

Robina had often wondered how he was.

She could remember him as a tall plain boy who was incredibly fond of horses, as she was herself, and who was forever getting his brother, Ellis, out of trouble.

Ellis had been born bad she reckoned and had not been seen locally for some time.

Ellis, it seemed, was in London.

Lord Hampton finished the water and then snapped his fingers. Almost immediately, his manservant was by his side.

"Fetch the carriage, Brocklehurst, we are returning to the castle."

The castle!

Robina longed to be asked to see it, but had heard from gossip that it was a shadow of its former self. The ageing Earl had not the time nor the money for it and it was said that its once-magnificent Tower was crumbling.

"You have to leave us so soon?" her mother was saying with a concerned look, "and you have barely had a chance to tell Robina about Robert's adventures in India."

"I am sorry, Lady Melville, but once the coughing comes upon me, I need to retire."

They watched as the Earl was helped away.

"Poor man!" sighed her mother, "he really is very unwell."

"And you, Mama – you are looking pale. I noticed it yesterday evening."

Robina took her mother's arm and looked into her grey-green eyes searchingly. It seemed as if the light had been extinguished in them. All her pain was visibly etched on to her face.

"I am fine, my darling," she answered with a smile, "you must not concern yourself unduly."

Almost as soon as the words were out of her mouth, a look of agonising pain crumpled her features.

"*Mama?*"

But she did not answer. She simply clutched at her stomach and folded in two.

"Is everything all right?"

It was Robina's father. He had been watching his wife closely all day and his eyes had not left her face for a second.

Upon seeing her wince he had rushed to her side.

"I must insist that you retire at once, Pamela."

"No, no, I will be fine in a moment. My guests – I must see to my guests."

Once again her face contorted in agony as the pain shot through her.

Robina could not help but start to cry.

'I must not allow Mama to see I am upset. I must not,' she said to herself as she turned away.

But the pain became too much and, eventually, she had been taken up to her room and the doctor called.

Robina was told by her father to remain downstairs and talk to the guests, but even as she laughed and smiled with them, she wished she was by her mother's side.

The party had come to an early end as the guests, sensitive to the plight of their hostess, drifted off before the sun set.

After Robina had said goodbye to the last one, she ran upstairs to be with her mother.

The grave look on her father's face had told her all.

"Darling, now you will need to be very brave, your

mother is never going to recover. The doctor has found a tumour in her stomach and they cannot operate."

At that moment Robina's world had fallen apart.

From that time on her dear mother was bedridden and the regular routine of nurses and doctors became a part of everyday life at Trentham House.

Robina gave up her studies and devoted herself to caring for her mother as best she could.

She was at her bedside when she died, holding her hand as the poor woman gasped for breath.

Robina cried as if her heart would break.

Nothing had prepared her for the complete and utter desolation she felt as her mother lay back on the pillow, still and lifeless.

*

But that was just a year ago and now Robina found herself returning to Trentham House in the family phaeton.

She sighed again as she huddled closer to Nanny.

They had now been travelling for over an hour and she noticed that Nanny had not said much about the house or her father, so finally she broached the subject.

"Nanny, how is Papa?"

"As I said before, he is much better than he was."

"And the house? Is it just the same? I cannot wait to see it again."

Nanny hesitated and could not meet Robina's eye. She gazed out of the window even though it was now dark outside and seemed to consider her words carefully.

"There have been many changes at the house," she said finally, "but you will find everything in good order."

There was a weighty silence as the carriage rattled along the road.

It was the same one that Robina had travelled in on her way to France, although she could see that the interior had since been reupholstered and the door handles were all brand new.

"Papa has been spending his money, I can see – " she remarked, hoping it might draw Nanny out of her shell, but the old woman remained silent.

'There is something much amiss here,' she thought, 'when I left for France, I commented about the state of the phaeton and Papa had said that it was not worth the money to refurbish! Usually, when Papa makes his mind up about something, he does not easily change it.'

Robina's thoughts turned to the family that she had left behind in Paris.

She had not wanted to go to France, but no amount of tears or pleading would change her father's mind.

A few days later, she had found herself en route to Dover, dreading what might lie ahead.

And then when she arrived in Paris, she had been so welcomed by the Lamonts, that, in spite of herself and her misgivings, she had soon found herself warming strongly to the family and their City.

"You will find that French gentlemen are different to the English," Nanny had warned her on the journey out. "You must be so careful not to take their words of love too seriously. For Frenchmen to flatter a woman is as second nature as breathing and I don't want you to believe you are in love with some charming rogue who is merely passing the time of day with you."

Indeed it had seemed to Robina that every man she met paid her compliments. She had not felt very attractive in her dull mourning clothes, yet she was constantly being told how lovely she was.

Even Jacques Lamont, the youngest son who was at least two years younger than Robina, had flirted with her and tried to snatch a kiss at a grand ball whilst they were walking in the gardens.

"Jacques!" Robina had cried, as he lunged at her by the fountain.

"I am sorry, Robina, but you see, you are just so beautiful that I had to kiss your lips."

"I shall have to tell your Papa if you do not behave yourself," she answered, trying hard to sound outraged as well as disguising a smile.

"Oh, Robina, *cherie*, you do not mean that," he had implored, inclining his head on one side pleadingly.

She had arrived in Paris as skinny as a colt and had left a curvaceous young woman.

She regarded her reflection in the carriage window. It was so dark outside that it was almost as reflective as a mirror.

Her face had now filled out and she had lost her 'pinched' look.

The Frenchmen had eyed her appreciatively when she had attended the opera dressed in her black silk gown with daring, short, puffed chiffon sleeves.

Whereas before she could never have worn such a gown as her shoulders were too bony, now she found she was drawing admiring glances.

During the course of her stay, Robina had become fluent in French and could easily hold a long conversation on almost any topic.

And to pass the time she had also applied herself to learning German and a little Greek.

She immersed herself in Parisian Society and came to know the Louvre well. She could hold her own in any discussion about art and became quite an expert on Rodin and went to great lengths to be invited to his studio.

Leaning over now to the seat opposite, she noticed a new cashmere blanket on it. She fingered the soft fabric and realised that it must have been rather expensive.

'How very curious,' she mused, 'this looks as if a woman chose it. It is far too subtle and delicate to appeal to a man's taste.'

"Nanny, who bought this cashmere blanket?"

Nanny coloured deep red and appeared flustered by the question.

"I could not – say," she stammered.

"Nanny, there is something odd about this. The new blanket, the new decorations in the carriage. I know that Papa has no interest whatsoever in this kind of thing."

She stared hard at the poor woman and she could see that she was visibly distressed.

Finally in a low voice Nanny blurted out,

"It is a new friend of your father's. She has been spending much time at Trentham House and she has made certain changes."

"A female friend?" gasped Robina, unable to take in what Nanny had just said.

"Yes."

"Papa has been entertaining a lady friend at home?"

"Yes."

Robina felt shocked – she could not believe that her father would be interested in the company of a woman so soon after her mother' death. Surely it would be innocent?

But Nanny's expression said a great deal and with a sinking feeling, it now occurred to her that this woman was possibly more than a companion.

She was beginning to feel uneasy at the prospect of going home. How would she possibly broach the subject with her father?

"Nanny," she began again. "Does Papa have many lady friends visiting Trentham House?"

"Not really, Robina,"

"Well, does this lady come for short visits or does she stay for weekends?"

Nanny grew uneasy and steadfastly gazed out of the window.

"I have said more than enough. You must ask your father."

"But Papa is not here, Nanny, and I wish to know!"

Nanny did not answer.

A sudden jolt threw Robina almost off her seat and, for the moment, she forgot all about her irritation.

"Are you all right, Robina, dear?" asked Nanny, as she helped her back into the seat.

Robina rubbed her arm.

"I think I am, but my arm is a little painful."

"Tch, you always were a clumsy girl. We shall get the doctor to look at it first thing in the morning," clucked Nanny, rubbing Robina's arm as if she was a small child once more.

Robina dozed off as the carriage rocked and seated next to Nanny with her familiar smell of soap and lavender, she was soon soothed.

As she slept, she dreamed all over again of the day that they buried her Mama.

It was a cold and wet day and the heavy mourning clothes she had donned were scratchy and uncomfortable.

She relived walking downstairs and glimpsing the

glass-sided carriage with the jet-black horses snorting and shaking their heads so hard that the ostrich plumes danced.

She could once again see the coffin draped in black velvet as it was carried to the hearse. Her father followed behind, his black silk top hat in his hand and a grim look on his face.

Then in her dream, she was suddenly standing by the open grave and, as she went to throw in the earth, she slipped and fell straight into the hole.

She tried to scrabble up the sides of the deep trench, but kept on sliding.

The trench seemed to grow deeper and deeper –

She shouted as the gravediggers started to shovel spadefuls of earth into the hole – but they did not hear her.

"Help! Help!"

Robina next awoke with a start and grabbed hold of Nanny's arm tightly.

"What is it? There, you were having a bad dream."

Nanny stroked Robina's hair and patted her hand.

Robina felt sick. She had been repeatedly having the same dream ever since she had first arrived in Paris and each time, she was convinced that she was about to die – suffocated in her own mother's grave!

"I was dreaming about Mama's funeral. It is always the same awful dream."

"You have not seen the monument, have you? It is a beautiful angel gazing up to Heaven, flanked by pillars. Your father commissioned a top architect to design it and one of the best masons in London carved out the figure. It bears your mother's likeness – "

"I would like to see it," murmured Robina, deep in thought.

She had not been to her mother's grave since she had left for France. It had still been a heap of earth when she last saw it and the first anniversary of her death was now looming.

It was nearly ten o'clock when the carriage finally turned into the driveway of Trentham House.

Robina's heart began to beat faster.

How would her father receive her?

Would he fling his arms round her and embrace her or would he merely nod and cough in that self-conscious way that he often lapsed into on emotional occasions?

The carriage pulled up at the front entrance and a footman came to open the door.

Robina did not recognise him, but had Nanny not said that some of the old servants had left because of her father's ill temper?

"Good evening, Miss Melville," he said, "welcome home."

"And you are?"

"Harrington, miss."

'It will feel so strange without Mama,' she thought, as she began to slowly walk indoors.

As soon as she was inside the hall, she noticed it.

Where the large Chinese vase had once stood, there was now an enormous French clock. Robina knew it was from Paris, as the Lamonts had something rather similar in their drawing room.

'This would not be to Papa's taste,' she reflected, as she took off her hat and gloves. 'It is far too ornate. Papa is much fonder of Chinese antiques.'

"Hallo, miss. Did you enjoy a pleasant journey?"

She spun round to see the familiar face of Newman, the butler, before her.

She sighed with relief.

"I am so pleased to see you, Newman!" she cried, "Nanny said that some of the servants had left and I would have hated it if you had been one of them."

Newman allowed himself a wry smile.

"It would take more than a few of your father's ill tempers to persuade me to leave Trentham House, miss."

Robina felt cheered immediately.

Perhaps things would not be so bad.

Nanny was still here and so was Newman.

"And my father – is he at home? I am eager to see him!"

It was all too obvious by the look upon Newman's face that there was something amiss. He gazed down at his highly polished shoes before answering.

"I am not certain as to his whereabouts at just this precise moment, miss."

Robina was aghast.

"Surely he knew of my return home this evening?"

"Of course, miss. That is why he asked Nanny to fetch you and not one of the footmen."

"You must know where he is, Newman. You know everyone's movements before they even know where they are going themselves. Is he not waiting for me?"

He sighed and gave Robina an almost pitying look.

"Sadly I am no longer privy to all of Sir Herbert's engagements."

Robina stared at him as if she could not understand the words.

'What on earth can he mean?' she said to herself. 'How can our own butler not know where the Master of the house is?'

She took off her coat and handed it to Nanny.

She did not know if she should run to the library or whether to go upstairs to knock on his bedroom door.

"You must be so tired, Robina," suggested Nanny. "Why don't you go up to your bedroom and I will ask for a tray with some supper to be brought to you."

Nanny could plainly see the turmoil raging within her, but she was powerless to help. Sir Herbert had made her promise that she would not say anything about the new arrangements until he had spoken to her himself.

"But I want to see my Papa!" she answered Nanny with her voice getting shriller.

"You will see him in the morning," said Nanny in a soothing tone, but Robina was in no mood to be placated.

She turned and grabbed Nanny by the shoulders, her fingers digging into her arms.

"Where is he, Nanny? Do you know? Why won't anyone tell me where he is?"

A noise at the top of the stairs made her look up.

With much hope in her heart that it was her father, she glanced up to see the figure of a woman in evening dress come slowly down the stairs towards her.

"You must be Robina – welcome home," mouthed the woman with very little warmth in her voice.

She could only stare disbelieving at the apparition walking towards her.

The woman was dressed in a green velvet dress in the latest style with large puffed sleeves decorated in black lace and dainty ribbon shoulder straps.

Around her neck glittered a necklace of enormous emeralds and she wore matching earrings. There was also an obsidian brooch set in gold at the front of her dress that was almost as large as a pullet's egg.

Robina's first impression was that she was terribly overdressed and that, although very beautiful, she was no longer a young woman.

"Who – who are you?" she now stammered, unable to take her eyes off the glittering figure who stood only feet away from her.

"Your father will explain everything to you. Now do hurry, he is waiting in the library – he has some news for you that I am certain you will want to hear."

Robina's heart hammered in her chest.

Her mouth felt dry and the prospect of seeing her father suddenly did not seem half as appealing.

"Come along," said the woman, beckoning for her to follow as she walked towards the library, "we are about to have dinner, rather late, I am afraid, and I know that he wishes to speak with you before it is served."

Mutely she allowed herself to be led to the library.

'Who is this woman who makes me feel a stranger in my own home?' she pondered, as she entered the library.

Her father was standing by the desk, looking rather healthier than he had the last time she had seen him. His cheeks had filled out and he had lost the haunted look that had blighted his face.

"Robina, I am glad you have come home again," he began, only meeting her eyes for a fleeting moment.

'There is something not right here,' she mused and did not know whether to approach him or if she should stay where she was.

She waited for him to speak, but the silence seemed interminable.

The strange woman in the evening dress crossed the room and went to her father's side.

There was something in the way that she looked up

at him – in mute adoration as if he was the centre of her world – that made Robina feel sick to her very stomach.

Her head spun and she grasped hold of a chair to steady herself. Not only was she feeling tired, but she was disorientated.

After speaking only French for so long, she was not certain that she really understood just what was happening as her father continued,

"Robina, my dear, there is something I need to tell you and I do want you to be very happy for me," he said at last, taking the woman's hand.

CHAPTER TWO

As Robina stood facing her father and the strange woman, it was if she was hearing what he was saying from a very long way away.

"Robina," he resumed, "I know how much you love me and that you would want me to be happy and I have to confess that since your dear mother died, I have been very lonely."

Robina opened her mouth to protest that had he not sent her away, then he might not have found himself in that unenviable state, but the words would not come.

"Laura has been a great comfort to me and I do not know what I would have done without her counsel and her company. So when I tell you that we were married just two weeks ago, I am certain that you will be pleased for me and will embrace your new stepmother and welcome her to Trentham House."

"No! It cannot be!" she cried, throwing her hands up to her face. "Mama has barely been dead a year – it is too soon. *Too soon!*"

"Now, my dear, is that any way to greet your new Stepmama?" chided Laura, looking at Robina as if she was just a petulant small child.

"Papa, *how could you!*" she shouted, throwing him a hurt look before turning and running out of the room.

Tears blinded her as she ran upstairs.

Unable to see where she was going, she plummeted

into Nanny who was carrying a large bundle of laundry.

"Robina. What on earth is the matter?"

"Oh, Nanny. Did you know that Papa had married *that* woman?"

"Yes, I did, dear, but I could not tell you. It was not my place. I don't agree with this hasty marriage any more than you do, but it has happened and so we must get on with life."

"But how could he? It is far too soon after Mama's passing."

Nanny ushered her into her room and put down her pile of laundry. She took a handkerchief from the dresser and handed it to her.

"Your father has been very much happier since her Ladyship came into his life and you want your Papa to be happy, don't you?"

"Yes, of course, but why did he have to send me away? If he had not done that, then perhaps he would not have felt it necessary to seek comfort elsewhere."

"My dear, men are not the same as us – they are not very good at being on their own. Whereas when a woman's husband dies, as my dear own Jack, we are able to carry on without a man around, but men need a woman to care for them, and I am not talking about a daughter!"

"Oh, Nanny! When Papa invited me home again, I did not think for one moment that I was going to feel as if I was an intruder in my very own home. This new woman – where has she come from? I did not see her at the house when Mama was alive."

"I believe she was married to one of your father's friends, who had died tragically a year before your Mama. Lady Wolverton, as she was then, went to Europe after the funeral and came back a year later to find your Papa was in the same boat.

"They were two lonely souls and then they found each other. Your Papa was so unbearable before she came into the picture – you should be grateful to her!"

"Nanny, do not say that – it makes me feel sick! *I* should have been enough for Papa and if he was lonely, he should have brought me back from Paris."

"My dear Robina, he found it too painful to look at you. Do you not know how like your Mama you are?"

"But Mama had grey eyes and I have brown," she replied, wiping hers with a soggy handkerchief.

"It doesn't matter to your Papa, you are the very image of her."

"I do not understand," sniffed Robina.

"You will when you fall in love," answered Nanny, mysteriously.

"Oh, I shall not fall in love with anyone."

Nanny laughed fondly.

"You have been saying that ever since you were a little girl. But you will one day, you wait and see."

"I cannot imagine that there is a man out there that would make me want to ignore my own child!"

"It happens, dear, it happens. Now dry your eyes. Your father will probably be upset that you were not more welcoming to her Ladyship. She can do no wrong in his eyes. Although I have to confess that no one can replace your Mama in my heart, this Lady Wolverton, as she was, has made him a happy man. Now it is late and I must take these downstairs for the morning. Good night, Robina."

"Good night, Nanny, and thank you."

"You will forgive me for not telling you about your Papa's new wife?"

"Of course, Nanny."

But Robina felt passionately that she would never understand why her father needed to remarry if she lived to be two hundred.

'Papa cannot love me any more otherwise he would not have married her. He must have deliberately kept me in France so that he could enjoy her company without the encumbrance of me around. Will he come to the cemetery with me on Saturday or will he drag that woman with him? Surely he would *not*?'

She walked to her window and peeped through the curtains. Outside it was very dark and she wondered what changes her stepmother had wrought in the garden.

'It must have been she who was responsible for the phaeton and that huge clock in the hall!'

She undressed and climbed into her bed – she was exhausted.

She thought of her stepmother and father enjoying an intimate dinner together.

'I hope I spoiled their appetites,' she grumbled and then immediately despised herself for being so ungenerous.

She still loved her father but this – this woman!

It was some hours before she eventually fell asleep. All she could think about was the strange new woman now living under the same roof.

*

The next morning, Robina feigned a headache and asked for breakfast in her room.

She was just taking the top off her first egg, when Newman knocked and came into the room.

"Excuse me, miss, but the Master wishes to see you in the library."

Robina put down her spoon and hesitated.

"Very well. Will you please tell him that I shall be down as soon as I have finished breakfast?"

"Yes, miss."

In the cold light of morning she bitterly regretted having behaved so hysterically the night before. She knew that her father could be an unforgiving man and she would have to throw herself at his mercy.

A few moments later she was downstairs knocking on the library door.

"Come in," came her father's deep voice.

She entered and threw herself down at his feet.

"Oh, Papa!" she howled, "I am so sorry for the way I behaved last night. Please, *please* forgive me!"

She dared not look up – she gazed at his shoes and noticed with some pleasure that he was wearing the hand-made leather shoes that her mother had given to him a few Christmases ago.

After what seemed like an age, her father took her by the chin and raised her face up to his.

"Do not kneel down on the floor, Robina, I expect that you were simply overtired from your journey and then you were overwhelmed by my news. Get up, please."

She rose up and her father took her hand.

"Oh, Papa, I missed you so much," she whimpered, as she tried not to cry.

"And I missed you, Robina. But you have to realise that my marriage to Laura is no reflection on my love for you. I was lonely and she helped me through a bad time."

"Why did you not ask me to return home?"

He sighed and toyed with a jotter on his desk.

"I am afraid I cannot explain my reasons to you, but I want you to know that I thought of you every day."

21

"But I am your daughter and my place is with you."

Her father looked up as if to say something just as his new wife came into the room.

"Ah, my dear, there you are. Good morning to you, Robina. I trust you slept well?"

'She speaks as if I was a guest in my own home,' Robina fumed to herself. She noticed that her stepmother did not wait for an answer to her question.

She was behaving, in fact, as if Robina was not in the room.

"Darling, I do hope you will be here for luncheon as I have asked Mrs. Bailey to prepare your favourite soup and there will be fresh peaches for pudding."

Robina looked at the way she was now caressing her father's arm – and in front of her!

'Mama would never have made such a spectacle of herself!' she thought.

Laura continued to ignore Robina's presence as she cooed and fluttered around her new husband.

"Darling, I must be going," said her father at last.

Robina looked up hopefully, but she was dismayed to see that her father was addressing his wife and not her.

He then bent forward and kissed her on the lips.

Robina shuddered and a chill ran through her heart.

'They make me feel invisible,' she thought, as her spirits sank ever lower.

As her father passed by on his way to the door, he threw a fleeting smile in her direction that made her feel as if she was begging for scraps.

She stood there, feeling a little awkward. She was aware that Laura had remained in the room and was staring quite hard at her.

As the door closed, she took a step forward towards Robina.

"I am glad that we are now alone, Robina, because I think it is only right that I should speak my mind as early as possible."

"Speak – your mind?" questioned Robina, not quite comprehending what she was trying to say to her.

"Yes, you must see, being alone so much with your father has meant that we have become very, very close – in fact so close that we do not need anyone else except each other. Do you understand what I am trying to say?"

Robina looked at her stepmother blankly.

"I must confess I do not," she said in such a quiet voice that it was barely audible.

"Robina, you are twenty and that is a dangerous age for a young girl. If you leave it too much longer then I fear you will not find a husband. I am the Mistress of Trentham House now and having two ladies under the same roof of equal rank is not a happy situation. I think you should now make every effort to find a suitable match."

"But I have no wish to marry yet."

"Nonsense, it is every young girl's dream!"

"It is not mine!" cried Robina. "And besides, Papa will never allow it. He has always said that I should marry for love and not for convenience or politics."

Laura smiled in a superior fashion.

"I think you will find that he is of the same mind as I am on this matter."

She held Robina's horrified glare without flinching. Surely what she was saying was not true?

"We shall see," was all she said before turning on her heel and walking out, leaving Laura on her own.

Robina knew there was only one place where she

could think properly and that would be galloping across the fields on the back of Firefly, her stallion.

'I should have gone straight to see him before I had breakfast,' she told herself, making her way to the stables.

"Miss Robina. We have been expectin' you."

Charles the groom put down the bridle that he was mending and walked towards her.

"Firefly has missed you! He hasn't been anythin' like his old self since you left us."

"I hope you have been exercising him regularly," said Robina, with a huge grin spreading across her lovely face. "He can be such a crosspatch when he is not given free rein across the fields."

"I've had young Jack take him out every day, miss. He's about the same height as you, although I think old Firefly knows the difference."

"I should hope so. I would be very disappointed if anyone else was to win his heart. Now, where is he? I am longing to see him."

Charles moved off towards the stable door and led Robina to a new stall towards the end of the building.

She noticed, as she passed the other stalls, that there was a new horse – a dapple-grey mare – chewing away on a bale of hale.

"Whose mount is that mare?" she asked, knowing the answer even before Charles could answer her.

"That is her Ladyship's, miss. Her name is Pearl. Not that her Ladyship has much time for ridin', the poor mare is no better than just decoration. Good job there are plenty of people to take her out to stretch her legs."

"She is so pretty – if Firefly would not get jealous, I should like to take her out sometime."

Charles chuckled as he held open the stall door.

"Old Firefly has quite taken a fancy to her, which is why we have put them in the next stall to each other. He's always had an eye for the ladies!"

Robina let out a loud cry of joy as Firefly poked his large black head through the stable door. He whinnied in response and appeared terribly excited to see his Mistress.

She threw her arms around the well-muscled neck and inhaled the familiar smell.

How sweet it was for her to be reunited with him.

"You handsome boy," she crooned, "I have missed you so much. And what is this I hear that you have found yourself a lady love? Shame on you! You should know by now I would be jealous. Perhaps I shall take her out riding today and not you!"

The horse nodded his head and appeared delighted at the attention.

"See, he has missed you, really, miss."

"Tell me now, Charles. Has Papa been out riding recently?"

"We have not seen him much, miss, save for when he comes to show visitors round. Perhaps now that you are back home, he will be tempted to go ridin' once more."

"Hmm," muttered Robina, "that is not like Papa."

Secretly she was thrilled that her stepmother did not have the same enthusiasm for equestrian sports, as it meant that she could share something with her father that she did not.

Robina stroked Firefly's nose thoughtfully.

"And Hercules, his mount? Is he well?"

"Aye, I reckon so. Misses his Master though."

Charles looked down, realising that perhaps he had said more than he should have done.

"Do not worry, Charles. I do not take what you say as disloyalty. Papa has just remarried, I expect his mind is not on his horses at the moment."

"Still, you are now back with us, miss, and no one except you and the Master can handle Hercules!"

Robina laughed softly.

The big old bay stallion was a handful indeed. But through much quiet patience and persistence, she had won his heart much to Firefly's consternation.

"I do not think that this fellow will forgive me if I take another horse out before he has a chance to feel the bit between his teeth. Come, let us take him and saddle him up. I feel the need to be out in the hills."

Charles shouted for Jack to bring the bit, bridle and saddle and as he did so, Robina heard a minor commotion at the other end of the stables.

"Oh, now what is it!" exclaimed Charles, shaking his head.

As he spoke, a handsome man on a chestnut horse came riding into the courtyard.

"I say, can you help me? My horse has lost a shoe and as I was passing, I thought you may be able to help."

Robina looked up the man.

His thick wavy brown hair and startling blue eyes put her in mind of someone, if only she could remember whom.

She watched him as Charles bent down to take the horse's hoof in his big hands.

"Aye, I reckon we can do it for you, my Lord!"

'My Lord?' thought Robina, staring at him.

The man jumped down from his horse and returned her long stare.

"Robina?" he called after a moment. "Is it really you? Could it be?"

It was then that she realised who the man was.

"Why, my Lord!" she exclaimed, laughing as the man picked up her and whirled her around.

"Goodness, how you are all grown up! Why, the last time I saw you, you were no more than a schoolgirl."

Robina blushed to the roots of her hair.

"It has been so long since I last saw you."

She looked at the tall handsome man before her and could scarcely believe that it was her old playmate, Robert, now the new Earl of Hampton.

"Yes, and I have been halfway around the world since then."

Remembering that he, as well, had suffered a recent bereavement, she said,

"I was so very sorry to hear of the death of your father. It was not long after Mama became ill, wasn't it?"

The Earl sighed and took on a pained expression.

"That is quite right. Father died in August and your Mama died the following year, did she not?"

"Yes, it is almost a year to the day."

"Oh, I am so sorry," said the Earl, reaching out to touch her shoulder. "But tell me, I had heard that you were in France, so when did you return?"

"A few days ago. But I am not the only one to have undertaken some travel, am I? I had thought that you were in India."

"I was forced to return home quite recently. After Father's death, I tried to keep my Army Commission and run the estate, but it was increasingly difficult. Ellis was never one for knuckling down to his duties and so, in order to prevent the house from falling into utter ruin, I returned home. For the past seven months the estate has kept me more than busy."

"Do you miss India? It must be a fascinating place – so colourful and exotic."

"It is indeed a wonderful country, but my place is at home. I have done my patriotic duty and with so much to do here, I did not feel it right to indulge myself playing at soldiers."

"But you were not playing, I am quite certain. Her Majesty's Empire has to be defended from the Russians."

"It is one long battle that will not be won overnight. They persist in attacking our borders, but we kept them all at bay."

Robina knew little of the current situation, but had heard talk of it in Paris.

She looked into his shining blue eyes and thought how clever he was. She did not remember him as being a particularly studious child, in fact, she recalled that he was most fond of sports and horses to the exclusion of all else.

Obviously he had changed a lot over the years.

As she watched him leading his horse to the smithy, she marvelled at how tall he had become.

The old Earl was a short stocky man and had never been particularly attractive even in youth. She had seen a portrait of him on horseback at Hampton castle.

'He must take after his grandfather or an uncle,' she mused, 'as the Countess was not a great beauty either.'

A few moments later and the Earl was back beside her as she stroked Firefly.

"So is this your stallion?" he asked clearly admiring the animal.

"Yes, it is. I missed him so very much whilst I was

in France. The Parisians do not seem to adore riding in the same way as we do, certainly the family I was staying with were not at all bothered about equestrian sports."

"And did you enjoy France? I must confess I have never visited Paris."

"I did not like it at first, but I came to love it. It is a very interesting City with plenty to keep one amused."

"Really?" replied the Earl, gazing at her lovely face intently. "Then I shall take your recommendation and visit Paris as soon as I can. Although I am not certain how soon that will be with my current plans for the castle."

"You are planning renovations?"

"Yes, much work needs to be done. My father was not interested in conserving the buildings and so it was left to crumble and the Tower is in a dreadful state.

"Thankfully, my Uncle Sebastian bequeathed me a great deal of money in his will when he died last year and I will be able to use it to pay for everything. I have a fancy to open up the castle to the public and hopefully this will make it pay for itself."

"That sounds just so wonderful!" enthused Robina, "I would dearly love to see the old place again."

"Then you must come and pay me a visit very soon. They say that the French have immaculate taste and I would be glad for your advice on the decor as you have been surrounded by nothing but the best for the past year."

Robina blushed.

She found it difficult to meet his eye and, although she had always called him Robert when they were children, she found it almost impossible to be so familiar now that they had grown up.

"I would love to," she murmured, casting down her eyes and blushing again.

They stood for some moments in awkward silence.

Finally Charles brought the Earl's horse back.

"There you go, my Lord – we've fixed his shoe and he's as right as rain now."

"Thank you, Charles."

The Earl mounted and smiled down at Robina.

"Do not forget – please come and visit me as soon as you are settled. I meant what I said about wanting your opinion."

"I will," she replied, shyly smiling back up at him.

With that the Earl spurred his horse into action and rode off with Robina watching him until he disappeared.

"He's a very fine man, the young Earl," commented Charles, as he opened the door to Firefly's stall.

"Yes, he is," mumbled Robina pensively.

As she led Firefly out of the stables, she was almost overwhelmed with an intense sensation of longing to see the Earl again very soon.

"Come on, my boy," she urged him, as she tried to push the Earl out of her mind.

But even as she rode across the rolling green fields, revelling in the sensation, the image of the handsome Earl refused to leave her mind for even a second.

CHAPTER THREE

As Robina galloped across the familiar countryside, she was filled with sorrow that her mother was not here to see it with her.

It had often been like this since her mother had died – she would see anything lovely or interesting, and the first person she would think of sharing it with would be her.

'And now she is no longer around and I miss her so much,' she reflected, as she stopped Firefly at a crossroads.

She paused to collect her bearings and realised that she was only a short distance from Hampton Castle.

"Come on," she urged Firefly, as she turned him in the direction of the castle.

Robina had no intention of paying a formal call, but her curiosity was now getting the upper hand as the Earl's description of his castle had fired her imagination.

'Perhaps if I ride around the perimeter, then I can gauge just how far the castle has deteriorated.'

It did not take her very long to reach the copse that overlooked the estate. It was on top of a hill and afforded her a panoramic view over the castle.

'Goodness!' she gasped, upon seeing that the top of the Tower had crumbled out and its castellated battlements were no more. 'It is worse than I had suspected.'

She recalled how, as a child, she and Robert would play *King Arthur* in the Tower – she would be Guinevere and he, Arthur. Ellis always wanted to be Lancelot and she remembered recoiling at such a prospect, as she had read in *Morte d'Arthur* that they were lovers and that meant that he might have to kiss her!

Ellis.

Were there ever brothers so incredibly unlike each other in just about every way? Ellis's hair was as black as pitch with brown eyes, whereas Robert's hair was golden brown and his eyes were startlingly blue.

Even as a boy there had been something somewhat unappealing about Ellis, who tended to be squat, while the Earl had been slender.

Robert had always been long of limb, whilst Ellis had a stunted look about him.

Ellis was the kind of little boy who enjoyed pulling legs off spiders and could never be trusted with an animal.

He had shown no interest in horses like his brother and, instead, preferred to lounge around the castle staring into space or sleeping.

In adolescence he had been something of a problem to his family. Once his brother had left for Sandhurst, he had thrown up any notion of education and had decamped to his father's flat in Mayfair, refusing to come home.

The old Earl, however, was inclined to indulge his younger son and considered it amusing that Ellis showed an aptitude for cards and had some luck at the races.

Thus Ellis had been spoilt and set upon the road to loose living.

Robina recalled before her Mama had died that she had eavesdropped on her father discussing Ellis with one of his friends.

One day she had gone into the library to pass the time and had been so delighted to find a shelf of books she had never seen before. She guessed by their titles that they had belonged to her mother, as she could not imagine her father reading *East Lynne* by Mrs. Henry Wood.

She crouched down and soon became immersed in the tale of murder and illicit love.

When her father had come in with Sir George Aird, she had not liked to get up – she always felt as if the library was special and that she must ask permission to be there.

So she hid thinking that they would not linger.

But they had.

"Yes, the boy has become a bit of a problem," she heard her father saying. "Since his father died, he has not grasped the nettle of his responsibilities and with the new Earl in India, I am deeply concerned that his conduct is not being corrected."

"I would imagine you have heard about his exploits in a certain theatre?" replied Sir George.

"I have and it is a shame I am not closer to him or I would take matters into my own hands and persuade him to see the error of his ways."

"This could be a huge scandal – a son of the House of Hampton cavorting with a Gaiety girl!"

Robina's ears had pricked up at this point.

Although she knew she was not supposed to know about them, she had heard all about the notorious chorus girls who paraded on stage at the *Gaiety Theatre* wearing daring costumes!

"Rumour has it that it was Constance Collier," said Sir George with a note of envy in his voice.

"He will bring great shame upon the good name of Hampton at this rate. Spending money as if it was water and frequenting common public houses."

"I heard that his brother has frozen his allowance," added Sir George.

"If he has any sense, then that is precisely what he should do and the sooner the better. However, my worry is for the estate. The old Earl did not leave it in good order and Ellis is running it on behalf of his brother."

"A spell in the Army would not go amiss," muttered Sir George darkly. "It has made a man of his brother."

The two men had then left the library together, so Robina had emerged from her hiding place.

"Well," she had exclaimed. "I am so very shocked. Ellis Hampton – a dissolute rake!"

And so as she now stood on the edge of the copse, she thought long and hard about the castle.

'Ellis must have spent all the money on high living in London,' she thought, as she squinted at several broken windows in the West wing. 'The gardens look bedraggled, even from this distance. They were always so beautiful – '

Suddenly she saw two figures at the bottom of the Tower and she hurriedly re-mounted Firefly and rode him deep into the trees.

'The last thing I would want is for the Earl or his awful brother to see me lurking around,' she said to herself as she turned Firefly around towards the main road.

The sun was at its height in the sky as she returned to Trentham House and the feeling in her stomach told her that it must be time for luncheon.

'I do hope that my Stepmama has gone out. I wish I could have luncheon with Papa alone.'

She ran upstairs to change and as she was buttoning up the nice clean linen blouse Nanny had left out for her, she heard the gong sound for luncheon.

As she descended the stairs, her stepmother walked towards her with a face like fury.

"Where have you been all morning, Robina? We did

not know whether or not to expect you to eat with us."

"It is of no consequence," replied Robina calmly, "Mrs. Bailey would have provided me with a morsel to eat had I not returned."

The expression upon her stepmother's face showed her utter disapproval.

Through tight lips she answered,

"Mrs. Bailey is not here to be at your beck and call. She gets very upset if people are not present for meals."

'That is not my experience of her,' thought Robina, although she wisely held her tongue.

"It is common courtesy to let us know whether you intend to eat with us," continued her stepmother, fuming. "Your father has faced enough problems with staff leaving and we certainly do not want someone as precious as Mrs. Bailey packing her bags just because you have been selfish and inconsiderate!"

Robina decided not to argue but, nevertheless, she was disappointed that she would obviously not be lunching alone with her father.

'My best form of defence is passive muteness,' she told herself, as her stepmother continued to berate her for her 'conduct'.

She simply cast her eyes down and appeared to be listening, all the while not taking in a single word.

In the dining room her father was waiting for them. His eyes lit up when he saw them arrive together.

"I am delighted to see that you are getting to know each other," he beamed.

Robina sat down and a plate of salmon was placed in front of her along with some boiled new potatoes.

She ate in silence as the pact between her father and stepmother made her feel as if she should not be there.

"I saw Lord Hampton today," she remarked at last. "He was saying that he has great plans for the castle."

"Really?" enquired her father. "I had heard he was back, but I must confess that I have not had the time to pay him a call. How is he?"

"He is well. His brother is causing him problems, however."

"The ne'er-do-well! Is he still spending the family inheritance?"

Robina laughed as she wondered if perhaps he had indeed noticed her crouched behind the sofa in the library that day!

"I believe he is attempting to, but the Earl is quite determined to renovate the castle. He has asked me to visit him to see what I think of his plans for the decor."

"Really?" interrupted Laura. "If it is advice about decoration that he seeks, then he should ask *me* – I am an expert – everyone who visits Trentham House remarks on my good taste."

Robina smiled and made no comment. The changes her stepmother had wrought were certainly not to her taste.

"Robina, there is one other matter I would discuss with you," continued Laura.

"Yes, Stepmama?"

"Your room is far too large for you and I intend to move you up to the blue bedroom on the top floor so that I can turn your room into a guest suite."

Robina looked up from her food in horror.

"But I have been in my room since I left the nursery and where should I bathe if I am in the blue room? There is no bathroom attached it."

"You will have a washstand and you can use the bathroom along the hall."

"But that is for the servants!"

"Then the servants shall have to use the washstands in their rooms and only use the bathroom once a week."

"Papa – " began Robina entreatingly.

But he was not looking at her. He stared resolutely down at his meal before speaking,

"You will do as your stepmother asks, Robina. We intend to entertain important guests in the autumn and we cannot make them use the blue room and the other rooms will not be remodelled in time."

Robina wanted to cry. She had been in her room with its lovely views of the gardens since she was three.

She put down her fork, unable to eat any more. The topic of conversation had quite made her lose her appetite.

"May I be excused," she whispered, trying hard to prevent tears from welling up in her eyes.

"Very well," agreed her father.

She was aware of her stepmother's glare as she left.

'Just how dare she!' she fumed, as she made for the garden, 'she will not be content until she has chased me out of the house!'

Robina noticed that a new fountain sparkled in the centre of the flower beds. This was one renovation of her stepmother's that she approved of, as she loved fountains.

It was an exact copy of a fountain in the grounds of Osborne House, Queen Victoria's holiday residence on the Isle of Wight, featuring a young boy entwined with a swan with jets of water that sprang up around them.

Robina sat on the narrow ledge and dipped her hand into the cool water and it soothed her immensely.

'I shall suggest to the Earl that a water feature in his garden would be most beneficial,' she mused.

As she sat there, she forgot about her troubles with her stepmother as her thoughts dwelled on the Earl.

'I don't think I would have recognised him if I met him in the street. He has grown so tall and so handsome.'

But romance was not something that concerned her – she had vowed to remain above such a notion in France and she did not see any good reason to cast that vow aside now she was back in England.

She told herself that her interest in the Earl of Hampton was strictly that of an old friend. In addition, she felt that he would understand her grief, having lost both of his parents.

'It grieves me to say it, but it is as if I have lost my Papa as well. He has changed so much since Mama died. I still cannot believe that he has married again so soon after her death – it is not right. I don't care what Nanny says about men being unable to be on their own – he is strong-willed and self-sufficient and this woman must have just inveigled herself into his affections!'

She was disturbed in her reveries by the sound of a cough and looked up to see Newman standing there.

"Excuse me, miss, we have been instructed to begin removing your belongings to the blue bedroom. Would you care to supervise the proceedings?"

Robina smiled at the faithful servant.

She had the impression that he did not care for his new Mistress either!

"Thank you, Newman, it is very thoughtful of you. I am quite happy for Nanny to supervise the move."

"Very well, miss."

He turned around and walked purposefully back to the house and Robina resumed her musings.

'So I am to be moved like so much luggage in spite of expressing a desire to remain in my old room.'

She stayed by the fountain for a time before going back to the house.

As she entered she noticed that her stepmother was departing in the newly refurbished phaeton.

'Perfect. Perhaps I can speak with Papa on his own at last.'

She hurried inside and made her way to the library, hoping he would be able to spare her a while to talk.

Her heart was beating as she approached the library door.

She knocked and after a few seconds, she heard her father's deep voice exhorting her to enter.

"Ah, Robina. This is an unexpected pleasure."

"Papa, we have not had any time alone since I came home and I wish to speak with you."

"I am rather busy this afternoon, my dear, can it not wait?"

Her face fell. Did he really no longer care for her?

He saw her expression and relented at once.

Laying down his pen he smiled at her indulgently.

"But yes, come, you are right that we have not been together since your return. Please stay for a while."

She felt as if she wanted to run to him and embrace him, but there was something in his demeanour to suggest that she should not. It seemed that he had quite a cold and unapproachable air about him – so unlike his old self.

"Papa," she began, "I am resigned to the fact that I shall have to move to the blue bedroom and I want you to know I shall not complain about the new arrangements."

"That is good, I am glad that you have seen sense," he replied delightedly. "Laura has put a tremendous effort into turning Trentham House into a modern residence. I do not want you to think I am doing it to erase all memory of your mother. No, that could never happen."

For a second he gazed off into the far distance and she felt that he did, indeed, still love her Mama very much. It heartened her to see his softened expression.

"But times are changing," he continued, "and Laura has reminded me that the house I live in reflects my status and being disinterested in such matters, I did not see what the colour of a wall or the style of the curtains would say to the world. Thankfully, she has educated me otherwise."

Robina nodded.

She was only too aware of how the Lamonts would judge a person by the furnishings in their house.

"So I am embarking upon this series of renovations and, once all complete, you will have a room that befits the daughter of a Knight of the realm."

"Thank you, Papa," answered Robina gratefully.

"Besides should your stepmother produce children, then we will need the nursery."

Robina's mouth fell open.

She had not considered that as a possibility.

"But Papa, forgive me for my boldness, but I had assumed Stepmama would not be interested in children."

What she really wanted to say was that she thought her stepmother too old to be of child-bearing age!

"She is still a young woman, Robina and it is a very real possibility. Much as I love you, a man desires a son so that he may pass his house and lands on to him as is right.

"You must understand that, being a female, if your stepmother has a boy, he will inherit everything. You will have to prepare yourself for that eventuality."

Robina sat still in stunned silence.

The notion had not even crossed her mind.

"That is how Robert Hampton inherited his estate. His elder sister was passed over when their father died and all went to him as the elder male."

"But Papa – it is so unfair!" remonstrated Robina. "Surely whoever may be the eldest should inherit the title and estate?"

He laughed indulgently at her.

"No, my dear, the law is inflexible on this fact. The eldest son, regardless of whether or not he is the eldest, is always the beneficiary. What do women know of business affairs or running estates?"

Robina felt that the law was not fair in the least and it made her realise just how unstable her situation had now become.

If her stepmother gave birth to a boy, she could find herself forced to live off his charity!

"But you will make provision for me?" she asked, her voice trembling.

Her father looked at her and shook his head.

"Robina, I would hope that when I come to die, you will be taken care of by your husband. Really, my dear, Laura is correct – it is time that you turned your attentions to finding a husband. I cannot devote so much time to you and it is only right that you seek someone while you are at the height of your attractiveness."

"But Papa, I have only just returned from France. I have barely unpacked and I want to stay here with you as long as possible."

He picked up his pen once more to signal that her audience with him was at an end.

"Don't be silly, you must consider marriage as soon as we find you a likely suitor. Laura is already scouring the best of London Society for suitable candidates and I trust you will be compliant with her wishes. I have no desire to be harbouring an old maid in my household!"

Robina felt shocked to her very core. She threw her hands up to her face and tried to compose herself.

'How could he! Just how could he!' she thought, as tears began to slowly run down her face.

Her father seemed oblivious to her distress. He was once more absorbed in his correspondence.

Turning away she left the library, crying silently.

She wanted to go to her room, but as she ascended the stairs, she noticed two footmen carrying her belongings up to the next floor.

She was about to turn around and go back into the garden when she saw Nanny coming along the corridor.

"Nanny," she cried out loud.

"What is it, Robina dearest?" she answered.

"Oh, Nanny. Papa does not love me any more!"

"Ssh, not in front of the staff," she counselled and led her into the morning room that was also on that floor.

Once inside Nanny closed the door and sat next to Robina on the blue silk chaise.

"Oh, Nanny! Whatever can I do? Papa is intent on marrying me off against my wishes. Firstly my stepmother makes it plain she does not want me here and now, Papa. I don't want to marry anyone, yet I feel as if I will be sent up the aisle at the very first opportunity. If and when I marry, I wish to marry for love and not for convenience."

Nanny patted her hand and helped wipe her eyes as Robina cried profusely.

"My dear, I don't know what to say to you. If your father wishes that you should marry, then that is his right."

"But it is *not* my desire!"

Nanny paused and then rose and left the room.

When she returned she pressed an old photograph into Robina's hand.

Tearfully, she looked at it – it was of her mother.

She stroked the image of the lovely young face with the wistful eyes.

"Mama would know what I should do now," she whispered, "if she was here, she would persuade Papa not to marry me off. They married only for love and I cannot understand why he will not allow me the same privilege."

Nanny touched her and again left the room.

Robina wept copious tears, stroking the photograph and raising her eyes to Heaven.

'If you can hear me, Mama, up in Heaven, then I implore you – help me! Look down on me and take pity!'

She stayed there for ages talking to her mother and hoping, praying for an answer or divine intervention.

Marriage to a man she did not love!

Robina felt she would surely die if she was forced to do so against her will.

'I will not allow it to happen to me,' she resolved, looking up to Heaven. 'Oh, Mama! Help me. Oh, how I *need* your love and advice.'

CHAPTER FOUR

The next day, Robina visited the florist to order the flowers for her mother's grave.

"Can it be a year ago?" asked Mrs. Bentall, the lady who owned the shop. "It does not seem possible and such a young woman. You must miss her terribly."

"Yes, I do. I am often frightened that I will forget Mama. There are times when I cannot recall what her eyes were like or her smile."

The woman nodded her head sadly.

"When I lost my own husband a few years ago, I experienced the self-same thing. But you do not forget – God gives us the strength to get through."

Robina felt somewhat comforted, standing in Mrs. Bentall's shop surrounded by beautiful blooms.

"And will you be placing the order for your father while you are here, too?" asked Mrs. Bentall.

"No," responded Robina, a little taken aback that he had not already made his own arrangements.

"Will you tell him that he must get his order to me soon if I am to supply the flowers he prefers? He was so particular with the funeral tribute that I would not like to disappoint him."

"Papa has much on his mind at the moment. I will remind him to pay you a visit."

After she left the shop, Robina wandered along the High Street. The village was fairly large, almost a small town and she knew every shopkeeper and tradesman in the place.

They smiled as she passed, said they were happy to see her again and it made Robina feel wanted.

'It's a fine thing when the village people make me feel more welcome than my own father,' she ruminated, as she climbed back into her carriage.

She asked the coachman to take her home.

As they drove along the road, they passed the gates of Hampton Castle.

'I must pay the Earl a visit very soon,' she decided, as they sped past.

*

Robina had not slept at all well in the blue room.

She had felt so cramped, although she had to admit that it was much easier for Nanny as she no longer had to walk up and down stairs to look after her.

'Poor Nanny,' she thought, as they arrived home at last, 'she is not getting any younger.'

She was so glad that Nanny had not been frightened off at the time when her father was at his most unpleasant.

She did not know what she would have done if she had returned to the house to find that Nanny had left.

Robina went straight to the library and saw that the door was shut fast.

She turned away disheartened. She had wanted to tell her father what the florist said about ordering flowers.

Instead she went to the drawing room and rang for Newman. She did not wish to involve her stepmother in this affair as she considered it none of her business.

After relaying the reminder for her father to order flowers to Newman, Robina went back upstairs.

The house no longer felt as if it was her home.

On the first floor, where her old bedroom had been, the builders were beginning their work. She had not asked her father to see the plans in case he had thought that she wanted to interfere.

'I do wish that Papa would confide in me as he used to,' she thought sadly, as she entered into her new room. 'I would have liked the opportunity to show him how much I learned whilst I was in Paris.'

She recalled how Madame Lamont had delighted in teaching her how to mix colours in decorating a room and how to create beautiful displays.

'The French have a way of putting things together that is effortlessly enchanting,' she pondered. 'If I cannot help Papa with his renovations and use my newly acquired talents, then perhaps the Earl will find them useful.'

She walked to her small desk and began to write a letter to him.

In it she said she intended to call on him the next morning and that she hoped it might be convenient.

She felt rather excited as she sealed the letter and then rang for Molly.

She was a new maid taken on to look after Robina, who only asked her to do things to save Nanny's legs.

Molly came in and bobbed a curtsy.

"Yes, miss?" she said, her sulky mouth pouting.

Molly was round and moon-faced with the distinct air of someone who carried out her orders under extreme sufferance.

Robina did not care for her, but, as she was never rude, she put up with her sullen attitude and slow ways.

"Would you see that this letter is delivered at once, please?" she asked, handing over the letter to Molly.

The girl bobbed another curtsy and took the letter without looking at it.

Robina was convinced that the girl was spying on her and reporting everything back to her stepmother, so the less she knew, the better.

Suddenly the future did not seem so bleak.

She would see the Earl and, if he should accept her offer, it would give her something to concentrate on.

'And maybe Papa will forget this nonsense about marrying me off. If he can see me visiting the Earl on a regular basis, perhaps I can use him as a smokescreen.'

A new plan was forming in her mind.

Surely her mother had come to her aid in giving her inspiration?

Feeling so much brighter, Robina went off to the stables to spend time with the horses.

'Yes, that is it,' she decided. 'I shall let Papa and Stepmama think that there is something between me and the Earl and then, perhaps, they will leave me alone.'

By the time she reached the stables, Robina was triumphant.

*

The next morning, Robina went down to breakfast to find a reply from the Earl waiting for her.

"*My dear Miss Melville,*" he wrote,

"*I would be very delighted to greet you today and although workmen are on site at present, I would indeed welcome the distraction and your wise counsel on points of decoration.*

Warm regards, Robert Hampton."

"Who is that from?" asked Laura, as she entered the room to see Robina engrossed in the letter.

"It is from Lord Hampton, asking me to pay him a visit this morning."

"I trust you will be home for dinner tonight," she responded tetchily, "we have an important guest."

There was something in her tone that suggested that there was more to it than just a simple dinner.

"Of course I shall," replied Robina, folding up the Earl's letter.

"Good," retorted Laura, "I have invited Lord Drury to join us and I want you to be extremely nice to him. He is a rich and powerful man whose wife has died recently, so he is looking for a new one. I think you will do him very well and I want you to look your prettiest."

Robina stared at her across the table.

"You mean me to encourage this man?"

"Yes, I do."

"And if I should not care for the gentleman?"

"It matters not whether you care for him or not – I am more concerned what he will think of you. Lord Drury would be such an ideal proposition for you and you would not want for anything."

Aghast Robina looked at her father for reassurance, but he would not meet her gaze.

'So I am to be sold off just like a prize heifer!' she thought, as she tried not to cry. 'Well, I cannot refuse to meet him, but I can refuse to marry him.'

Robina remained silent for the rest of the meal.

She felt that her best course of action was to appear to agree while silently rebelling. Besides if the gentleman proved to be interesting and kind, then perhaps she could take him into her confidence and he would not press her to marry him against her will.

After breakfast she changed quickly into her riding habit and before long was on her way to the stables.

"Good morning, Charles," she called out brightly, as she watched him fasten Firefly's bit and bridle.

"Morning, miss. I think he's ready for the off. I swear he knew last night, he was that restless."

Even as she rode off, Robina felt happier than she had done since she had returned home.

The very concept of involving herself in the Earl's renovations was exciting and it would certainly occupy her mind far better than dwelling on the appalling prospect of the evening's dinner.

Arriving at the castle, Robina noticed that the place was a hive of activity. The builder's cart was in evidence, as were numerous workmen.

As she led Firefly round to the Earl's vast stables, she passed by the Tower in time to see the Earl and another gentleman emerge from the base of it.

"Miss Melville!" he cried, waving enthusiastically.

He said something to the man next to him and then ran towards her.

"Good morning. How beautiful you look today!"

Robina felt herself blushing – there was something in the way that the Earl looked at her that unnerved her.

He gazed deep into her eyes and held his gaze for longer than was strictly necessary.

"Come, take Firefly to the stables and then join me in the drawing room. I shall be finished shortly and I can show you my plans."

He seemed as excited as a young child at Christmas and Robina admired the way he seemed to be so much in charge of everything.

She settled Firefly into a comfortable stall and then made her way to the front of the house.

It had been quite some years since she had last been inside and she was shocked at the deterioration she saw.

The wallpaper in the hall was peeling and had damp patches.

The Persian carpets were dirty and needed mending and she could smell an unpleasant mustiness.

Many of the fabrics were faded and threadbare and the furniture looked as if it needed a good polish.

She walked into the drawing room and it was not much better. The stones on the fireplace were chipped and there seemed to be loose floorboards wherever she trod.

'Goodness!' she murmured.

At that moment, the Earl entered the room with the man who had been outside earlier.

"You will not mind if Mr. Garnett and I finish our business in here, do you? You may find it interesting to hear what we are discussing."

He now spread out his plans over a large mahogany table and began to discuss with Mr. Garnett whether or not to remodel the drawing room.

"The fireplace is in great need of repair and I am debating whether or not to have it demolished and a new one installed. Also the French doors are rotting, perhaps they should be replaced with ordinary windows?"

"Oh, no!" cried Robina, "don't you wish to be able to see into the garden? This room requires as much light as possible as it is East-facing. I would think that it only gets the sun in the morning and becomes dull by lunchtime."

The Earl looked at her in astonishment.

"You are quite correct and so, you believe that with normal windows, the room would feel gloomier?"

"Quite so," answered Robina confidently.

"Then I will have new French windows built. And the fireplace, what would you suggest?"

Robina walked over and stroked it.

"This is Portland stone, isn't it? And very old. I do not think that a modern fireplace would be at all suitable. A stonemason may be able to redesign it and make it good. It would be a pity to lose such an intriguing feature."

"Then that is exactly what I shall do," declared the Earl, smiling at her.

He returned to the builder and they discussed more improvements with Robina adding her own suggestions.

After a few moments Mr. Garnett departed and the Earl rang for tea.

"Thank you so much," he said, sitting down in the chair next to her, "your advice has been invaluable. I recall that you always had an eye for design, but I can see that your time in France has improved it."

Robina looked at him with a puzzled expression.

"I cannot think of what I did as a child to impress you – "

"Your designs at Christmas and for all our birthday parties! Do you not recall how my Mama used to get us children to make decorations for the Great Hall? Yours were always so much better than anyone else's. You had a talent for it even back then."

She reddened and was grateful when Marriott, the Earl's butler, brought in the tea.

"Now," said the Earl. "Tell me what you think of the designs for the Tower."

He brought out another massive sheet of paper and spread it out in front of her.

It was a complex design that remodelled the Tower, whilst still being in keeping with the style of the house.

"It is very interesting," she remarked, after studying it, "but I notice that you have not planned to install electric lighting."

The Earl looked thoughtful for a moment.

"It is true that I want to have it put in to some of the rooms in the main part of the castle, but I had not thought of the Tower."

"Surely, it would be most beneficial? I remember the rooms being dark as there are only mullion windows in the walls. It would not cost a great deal to install it, if you are already building a generator for the main house."

"Thank you. It is such a brilliant idea," enthused the Earl. "I had no idea that you understood such matters."

"The Lamonts were very progressive and they got rid of their gaslights some time ago in favour of electric."

"I want the castle to become the most modern and progressive building in the country! Furthermore, I have yet more plans for it once it is finished."

"And what might they be?" she asked, intrigued.

"I want to open the castle to the public and host luncheons and teas for the well-to-do. These renovations will all but drain my spare funds and I need to maintain the buildings and the grounds.

"I have heard of other families opening their houses to the public and so thought that the castle would prove to be interesting for tourists. However, it is a part of my plan that will have to wait for some considerable time."

"Why? Although you have missed this year, surely you will be ready to welcome guests next year?"

"No," he sighed, "I do not have the time to write the letters and organise the whole thing."

"I could do it all for you!" cried Robina. "Let me be your secretary. I have nothing to do at home now that my new Stepmama is running the house and I could work with you so that as soon as the renovations were complete, you could begin to welcome guests.

"And with my French connection – why stop at just English visitors? I speak fluent French and could conduct the tours myself. I also know German and could easily learn other languages."

"Would you really?" he asked cautiously. "I would not dream of asking you to work for nothing and naturally, I would pay you."

"It would be *my* pleasure," she replied, believing this to be the answer to her prayers.

Working for the Earl at the castle would provide the perfect backdrop to her make-believe courtship.

"Papa may insist upon a chaperone. Could I bring Nanny with me?"

"If it is a problem I am sure that Mrs. Osidge would be grateful of the company."

Robina did not like to tell him her ulterior motive – at least, not yet.

"Then it is all decided. When would you like me to start?"

"Well, there is a huge pile of letters in my study to be answered if you would care to begin at once."

Robina sprang up from her chair,

"Lead me to them and I shall begin now."

Very soon they were in his study going through an endless pile of correspondence.

Robina looked at each one, asked for his response and then set to work on a reply.

'I had quite forgotten how well we used to get on,' she thought to herself, as they made idle chatter.

"So, tell me more about your time in France," asked the Earl later, as they ate luncheon.

"Oh, it was not as exciting as your sojourn in India, I'll be bound," answered Robina laughing. "I think it is I who should be asking you about *your* adventures."

"Oh, I don't wish to talk about any action I saw, but India is such a fascinating place. Did you know that they worship elephants and cows?"

"I cannot imagine it."

"The Hindus worship a God called Ganesha, who is represented by an elephant and they view a cow as sacred."

"Although I am fond of cows, I just cannot imagine viewing them as holy relics!"

"It is fearfully hot, too – unimaginably so. I found having to wear such a heavy uniform most uncomfortable."

"I have heard that the Indians experience the most dreadful rainstorms. Enough to drown a man."

"You are referring to the monsoon, no doubt. They do not have rain-showers as we do. At certain times of the year they have torrential rains that do not cease for days. That was almost as unpleasant as the extreme heat."

"I do not think I would care to live in India," said Robina, as they returned to the Earl's study.

"It has so much to recommend it – the temples, the animals, the superb scenery and the colourful people. The women particularly wear wonderful gowns so unlike those that British women wear."

Robina now sighed to see that the pile of letters did not seem to have abated in the least.

"Tell me," she asked, "how long is it since you last answered your correspondence?"

The Earl gave her a sheepish look.

"It is some months because the estate has kept me so busy and then, there was that trouble with Ellis – "

His voice trailed off as he stared into space.

"Ah, yes, Ellis. Where is he at present?"

"In London again."

"It must grieve you to have a brother who does not seem to care for the castle and estate as you do."

"It does indeed. I have not dared visit the Mayfair apartment for ages, as I cannot face the inevitable scene of destruction. I intend to see it only once I have finished the renovations on the castle.

"As far as I am concerned, unless Ellis attempts to sell it or stake it in a card game, which he cannot legally do as it is in my name, then I will not interfere."

"I often used to wish that I had a brother or sister," sighed Robina, "but hearing all your experiences makes me glad I am the only child."

"Alicia, my sister, never caused any trouble," added the Earl, "but I often wonder what would have happened to her after Father's death had she not married well."

"Such is the lot of female children," sighed Robina, trying to ignore the nagging fear that her stepmother might well give birth to a son.

"But you could have no concerns in that direction, surely?" asked the Earl, as if reading her thoughts.

She remained silent – could she tell him her worst fears?

"Your new stepmother – how old is she?"

"It is hard to say."

"I see," said the Earl, thoughtfully and then added, "and is she pleasant?"

"She certainly has not taken to me. In point of fact, she is making every effort to ensure I do not remain long under the same roof as her!"

"Why is that?" he enquired, sounding horrified.

"I wish I knew what I had done to offend her. Why, even as I sit here, she is busy planning to marry me off to some old rich man so that she can have Papa to herself!"

"You are too harsh. I cannot imagine how anyone would take against you so."

"I am telling you the truth. This very evening, she has invited some recently bereaved Lord to dinner so that he may consider whether or not I could be suitable wife material."

"That cannot be!" he exclaimed with an angry look on his face. "She cannot force you to marry against your will."

"Sadly I have no choice in the matter. I must do as Papa tells me and if that is marrying someone against my wishes – whom I do not love – then I have no choice in the matter."

The Earl brooded thoughtfully whilst she continued to sort out his letters and eventually, he spoke,

"I do not approve of arranged marriages. I believe that one should only marry for love and there should be no other reason. Father was also most resolute on this score – he told us all that although he wished us to marry to ensure that the family line continues, he did not expect us to marry for that reason alone."

"My Mama and Papa were a love match and I had hoped to make the same. I cannot understand why Papa is allowing Stepmama to follow this course of action."

"Perhaps she has persuaded him that it would be for the good of the family."

"I could not say, all I know is that I am terribly unhappy about it and if I can find a way around it, I will."

The Earl looked as if he was about to speak and then hesitated.

"No matter," he said, before returning to his plans.

Robina wondered what it was that he had wanted to say, but did not press him.

*

Before she knew it, it was almost time for dinner.

"How the afternoon has flown," she exclaimed, as Marriott came to tell her that Firefly was ready and waiting for her. "But I must take my leave as I have to be ready for this odious dinner."

"You are welcome to stay and have dinner with me, here at the castle," suggested the Earl with a hopeful air.

"No, that would cause too much of an argument. I must go home."

"I will see you tomorrow then."

"At nine o'clock, sharp," she replied, attempting to raise her own spirits.

She was dreading the return to Trentham House and would have far rather dined with the Earl.

As she was about to leave, the Earl said,

"My guest room is at your disposal should you ever require a place to stay. There could be times when I will need you to stay late or to start early and it would be most convenient for you."

Robina smiled gratefully, although she doubted that she would ever be allowed to stay with the Earl as a guest now that her stepmother had plans for her.

"Thank you," she replied, wishing she could stay.

Outside a well-rested Firefly was awaiting her. He shook his head and snorted as she appeared.

"See how eager he is to gallop across the fields.

He knows that he has a warm stable and hay waiting for him at home."

The Earl shook her hand warmly and thanked her again.

Robina felt that he appeared reluctant to let her go.

She mounted Firefly and rode off down the drive.

Had she looked back, she would have seen a wistful look on the Earl's face and the way that he stayed outside, watching her, until she disappeared from view –

CHAPTER FIVE

Robina arrived back at Trentham House with barely half an hour to spare.

She ran into the house in time to see her stepmother descending the staircase, dressed in one of her finest gowns and festooned with so many jewels that she glittered like a chandelier.

"Just why are you so late?" she snapped, as Robina drew level with her on the stairs. "Go upstairs at once and dress in your very best gown. And I want you to wear the diamonds I have had Molly put out for you – hurry, she is waiting to dress you."

"But only Nanny helps me dress – "

"Nanny is too old. If she is to be your companion, it is another matter entirely. No, Molly will see to it."

"But I do not want Molly – "

"There is to be no argument – we do not have the time!" cried her stepmother.

Robina became upset by this latest turn of events.

'What will happen to Nanny now?' she wondered, as she entered her room to find Molly bustling around.

"Your bath is now ready and drawn down the hall, miss," she mumbled in her dull voice.

Robina shuddered.

After her bath she changed as quickly as she could into her lilac-velvet dress with the extra long sleeves and high bodice. She deliberately decided not to wear her pink dress as it showed too much flesh.

'I don't want to feel vulnerable,' she thought, 'and I will not feel at all comfortable if I think that Lord Drury is peering down my neck!'

She sat in front of the mirror and had to patiently explain to Molly how she wanted her hair done.

Unlike Nanny with her deft fingers, she was clumsy and took an age to do it. She also pinched Robina's ears when she tried to put in the heavy drop-diamond earrings.

"So sorry, miss," she said, as Robina flinched. "We want you to look nice tonight, don't we? Madam says that there is a special guest tonight. An important gentleman, by all accounts. Madam says he is very interesting and has a great deal of money."

Robina forced a smile, but did not reply.

"I would count myself lucky if I were to meet such a distinguished gentleman," continued Molly. "I hear he has three houses – one in Biarritz, one in London and one in the County. And then there is his big stable of racehorses."

"Molly, I do not care if he is the Prince of Arabia!" interjected Robina impatiently.

It was obvious that her stepmother had primed the girl to extol Lord Drury's virtues.

"I was only saying, miss – "

"I would prefer it if you concentrated on my hair, thank you," insisted Robina firmly.

At last the gong sounded and Robina was relieved to get away from the girl.

"Do not worry about attending me before bed," she called as she was leaving. "I will see to things myself."

"Goodness!" cried Robina, out loud. "If I am forced

to have that girl attending me I shall go quite mad! I must ask Papa why I cannot have Nanny back."

She checked her reflection again in the small mirror and could see how the diamonds gave her skin a luminous sheen and she wished she did not have to wear them.

'I don't want to appear too attractive,' she thought, gloomily.

Taking a deep breath, she descended the stairs and walked towards the drawing room.

She went inside and, at once, saw Lord Drury.

He was just as she had feared – quite an old man, with snowy-white hair and a rotund figure. His hair stood on end as if he had been struck by a bolt of lightning and his face was florid and chubby.

"Ah, here she is," announced her stepmother. "Lord Drury, this is my stepdaughter, Robina."

Lord Drury turned around and his rubicund face lit up as he took in Robina from head to toe.

He struggled to his feet and Robina could see that his waistcoat was straining at the buttons.

She tried her best not to show her distaste, but she realised that her expression often gave away her innermost thoughts.

"Charming! Quite charming!" gushed Lord Drury, as he held Robina's hand and planted a slobbery kiss on it.

She withdrew her hand as soon as possible without causing offence, but if there had been a napkin to hand, she would have needed it.

Her stepmother watched her like a hawk as Robina walked to a seat as far away from Lord Drury as possible.

"Robina, his Lordship was just telling us all about his new stable of racehorses. I told him that you adore to ride," said her stepmother, just daring her to contradict her.

Robina managed a thin smile and looked down.

She refused to be drawn into the conversation.

"I used to ride a lot myself," added Lord Drury, smiling away at Robina, "but not in recent years, I admit."

"My horse has not seen me for many a long month either," added her father. "Poor Hercules!"

"He misses you, Papa," came in Robina, seizing the opportunity to turn the conversation away from herself.

They were interrupted by Newman, who came in to announce that dinner was waiting to be served.

Lord Drury took the opportunity to heave himself out of his chair and made a beeline for Robina.

"Accompany me into dinner, won't you, my dear?" he suggested, leering at her.

Robina took hold of the proffered arm and tried not to shudder.

She could see her stepmother smiling in triumph as they walked towards the dining room. In her head, Robina was almost halfway up the aisle.

In the dining room, Robina was given a place next to Lord Drury, much to her horror.

"You must tell me all about yourself, my dear," he began, as they sat down.

"Oh, there is nothing much to impart."

"Your father has told me that you have spent some considerable time in Paris – wonderful City."

"Yes, it surely is," she answered, staring down at the *consommé* that had been placed in front of her.

"I have friends in Montmartre – do you know it?"

"Yes."

"Robina, dear, tell Lord Drury about the Lamonts," prompted her stepmother, flashing a warning glare at her.

"They are some friends of Papa's," she offered and then fell silent.

In spite of her best efforts, Lord Drury continued to attempt to draw her into conversation. He talked at length about his horses, and then his house in London, and then his friendship with Lord Salisbury –

Robina did her best to stifle a yawn as the plates of the main course were taken away.

"A very fine sirloin of beef," declared Lord Drury, who had eaten several large helpings.

'It is no wonder he is as round as a ball!' thought Robina, as her half-eaten plate was removed.

"My wife, God rest her, loved her food. I cannot be doing with women who don't like to eat. To eat is to live," he boomed.

"I confess I do have the appetite of a bird," replied Robina, feeling pleased to have something with which to discourage him.

"Ah, that will all change when you marry and wish to please your husband."

"It is true," added Laura, "since Herbert and I have married, I have eaten like a common field hand. I put it all down to being happy."

She smiled at her husband and reached out to touch his hand. Robina felt her stomach lurch at this distasteful display of affection.

It did not seem right that someone other than her mother was making a fuss of her Papa.

"Robina has been spoiled by the fancy ways of the French. I must write to the Lamonts and chastise them."

"That is not so, Laura," said Sir Herbert suddenly, "look at Robina. She left the house as skinny as a newborn colt and returned a young woman."

The way he looked at her with obvious pride made Robina's heart swell.

'Perhaps Papa does still love me,' she reflected, as she smiled back at him.

Determined to spoil the moment, Laura jumped in,

"She could still do with gaining a few pounds – no man will look at her if she is too thin. Tell us, Lord Drury, do you think she is too skinny?"

Robina felt the man's hot eyes upon her, raking up and down her figure in the most nauseatingly fashion.

She could not help herself reddening with a mixture of shame and embarrassment.

Was it not enough to be paraded in front of him as if she was for sale?

"Far from it," he murmured, his heavy-lidded eyes full of pleasure.

Robina attempted to turn the conversation round to a different topic.

"Papa, I spent the day with Lord Hampton and saw his plans for the castle. I think you would be interested in seeing what he is planning as you are working on changes here at Trentham House."

Her father's eyes lit up as he was fond of discussing architecture and buildings.

"Really? I would like to see what he intends to do with the old place. I am so happy he is giving it his full attention, unlike that brother of his! I am quite certain that his father is looking down from Heaven and rejoicing."

"The Earl has asked me to help him with his plans to open the castle to tourists," supplied Robina, hoping that her father would not object.

"I am glad that you shall have something to occupy you. I had feared that, after Paris, you would find Surrey very dull. It is good that you will learn something of the value of money if you are earning your own."

"This is only a temporary measure, I would hope?" snarled Laura, "You should be looking forward to marriage and children and a house of your own, after all."

She glared at Robina, daring her to contradict her.

Robina fell silent.

"Quite right," added Lord Drury, "women working! Whatever next? I would die rather than send any wife of mine out to work!"

"But, Lord Drury, a woman would not need to think of lifting a finger if she was married to you," cooed Laura, in an attempt to sweeten the conversation.

Robina shuffled in her seat.

'I wish she would refrain from discussing the topic of marriage,' she fumed, just as the strawberry tarts were brought in.

Dinner seemed to drag on forever as Robina waited in vain for her father to request that the port be served.

Eventually after the conversation began to dwindle, Lord Drury asked Sir Herbert if he might have a word in private.

"Please come into the drawing room and I will ask Newman to bring the port and cigars through."

They all rose and Robina suddenly felt as if her legs would give way.

She had an awful sinking feeling that the reason for Lord Drury's request of a private audience was an ominous one.

Once they were alone Laura grabbed Robina by the arm and looked hard into her face.

"In spite of your best attempts to make yourself as

uninteresting and unattractive as possible to Lord Drury, I do believe that he is rather taken with you. I would hazard a guess that he is, at this precise moment, asking for your hand in marriage. A man like him does not linger once he has made up his mind."

"I will not marry him!" Robina cried out, almost in tears. "*I will not*!"

"You will do exactly as you are told," snapped her stepmother, gripping her arm so tightly that her fingers made angry red marks.

Just then Newman walked in, so she let go.

"Now, you will smile and look pretty," she hissed, "Don't let us down."

'I am surely walking to my doom,' thought Robina, as they moved towards the drawing room.

She could see that Lord Drury and her father were laughing and smoking and two glasses of port stood on the small mahogany table by the sofa.

"Ah, ladies," beamed Lord Drury.

"Robina, my dear," began her father, "Lord Drury has something to ask you."

With every fibre of her body taut she forced herself to move towards him as he leered up at her from his chair.

"My dear, I am in the habit of taking my carriage out in the early mornings for a breath of fresh air. Would you care to accompany me tomorrow morning?"

"I am very sorry, but I just cannot. I shall be busy working."

"What nonsense!" cried Laura angrily. "Don't pay any heed to her fanciful notions."

"I have been engaged by Lord Hampton to work as his secretary and he is expecting me to be at the castle first thing."

"You will write to him and inform him that you are

unable to visit him tomorrow and that is now the end of it," snapped Laura. "Now gentlemen, would you care for some more port?"

Robina was left sitting there feeling powerless.

'This is a clever game my Stepmama is playing,' she reflected, 'she thinks that if she embarrasses me, I will concede defeat. I have no intention of doing as she says!'

"Do come and sit beside me, my dear," suggested Lord Drury, patting the sofa next to him.

Robina smiled as best she could, but she felt sick to her very stomach.

His presence revolted her.

'The Earl said that if ever I should need sanctuary, then he could provide it. I shall make certain that I am not in the house tomorrow morning when Lord Drury arrives,' she determined, as a plan formed in her mind.

*

Robina made her excuses and left to retire to bed as soon as she could.

She allowed Lord Drury to kiss her hand and she smiled thinly as he told her that he would collect her at ten thirty sharp the next morning.

Although she had asked Molly not to stay up, when she arrived in her room, she was turning the bed down.

'Heavens. Can I have no privacy?' she moaned to herself.

"Shall I help you, miss?" Molly asked.

"No, thank you."

Molly bobbed a curtsy and then, after lingering for a split second by the door, she took her leave.

As soon as she heard the footsteps die away down the corridor, Robina locked her door.

Quickly she took down a small bag from the top of her wardrobe and began to put clothes into it along with a facecloth and some handkerchiefs.

'I shall wait until everyone is in bed and then I shall make my escape,' she told herself.

She sat and read until she heard the house fall silent and the clock struck one. Then, as quietly as she could, she changed into her riding habit.

Within a few moments she was creeping down the back stairs, hoping that none of the servants were still up.

The kitchen was quiet and dark as she reached the bottom of the stairs. She tiptoed into the main pantry and unlocked the back door as quietly as she could.

Outside the backyard was quiet. A bright moon lit her way across the garden and to the stables.

The horses had already sensed her coming and were shuffling in their stalls. She knew that Jack often slept in with the horses and she had come prepared.

As she opened the door to Firefly's stall, the horse snorted at her in greeting.

As she patted his forelock, she looked down to see the tousled blond head of Jack, as he lay on a pile of straw.

Taking a sixpence from her purse, she crept over to the boy and gently shook him.

"Jack. Jack," she whispered. "Wake up!"

The boy was soon awake and jumped to his feet.

"Sorry," he yawned, thinking he had overslept.

"Ssh, now listen carefully. I want you to saddle up Firefly for me, but you must promise me that you will not tell a soul. Look, here is sixpence for your trouble."

The boy gazed at the silver coin and without saying a word went and fetched the bridle and saddle.

"Now, go and sleep with Peony – she is docile and will not mind your being there. If Charles asks you about this, say you were so tired that you did not stir all night."

"Yes, miss," answered the boy, looking scared.

"Don't worry, you will not get into any trouble. I will make certain of that."

Robina led Firefly out of the stables and mounted him in the yard.

Within moments she was riding out along the dark road to the castle.

*

Although the moon was now bright, she had never ridden alone at night and found she was more frightened than she thought she would be.

The trees seemed to loom up menacingly in front of her, while the wind whipped her hair from under her hat.

By the time she reached Hampton Castle, she was dishevelled and freezing. She had not realised how much colder it would be at night and she had forgotten to wear her gloves.

Everything was silent as she rode into the courtyard that led to the stables.

The only sounds to break the cool night air were the snorting of horses and the snoring of the stable boys in the hayloft.

She quickly found an empty stall for Firefly before making her way to the castle.

Her first inclination was to try the French windows, but, feeling that was too much like breaking in, she decided to try the back door to the kitchen first.

She crept around the corner and found to her great surprise that the kitchen door was wide open.

'How very odd,' she mused, as she slipped inside.

She stood for a moment in the pitch-blackness and tried to find the electric light switch on the wall. Then she noticed a large oil lamp and a box of matches.

'Perfect. I will leave my bag here and explore. I seem to recall that the guest rooms are on the ground floor from the days of the old Earl's large hunting parties.'

As she crept along, the lamp threw up shadows and made her start.

The castle was eerie at night and as a little girl she had heard tales of a resident ghost.

Feeling her way she passed by the Earl's study and followed the corridor around.

'I am sure that the guest rooms are just a bit further along,' she muttered, as she felt her way along the wall.

The floorboards began to creak under her feet and there were strange noises at every step.

More than once she stopped to look around, feeling certain that someone was watching her.

That feeling grew stronger as she at last found the guest rooms.

'Ah, this must be the green room,' she thought, as she pushed open a half-ajar door.

This room was elegant and plush. By the flickering light of the lamp, she could see that it was well cared-for and appeared not have suffered any deterioration.

'To think, in its heyday, this wing would have been filled with up to fifty guests!'

A noise out in the corridor made her start and she nervously went to investigate. She opened door after door, but found only furniture swathed in white sheets.

'It would appear that only the green room has been made ready,' she observed, as she closed yet another door. 'Perhaps the Earl has had it put in order for me?'

The feeling that she was being watched grew even stronger, so she quickly returned to the kitchen for her bag.

She could not help looking over her shoulder as she went and the hairs on the back of her neck stood up.

'I would hate to see a ghost – even if it was Mama,' she murmured, trying to walk noiselessly on the tiled floor.

As she balanced her bag in one hand and the lamp in the other, she made slow progress along the corridors back to the East wing.

Eventually she reached the green room again and as she was feeling very tired she wanted to go to bed.

But something was not right.

She paced around the room and decided that it was because the room was too stuffy and warm. So she walked over to the French windows and undid the latch.

Swinging open the doors the night air gusted in and blew back the curtains.

For a short while Robina stood there with the cool air fanning her cheeks.

"Oh! I am so very tired," she cried out, as the wind tugged at her hair.

Pulling off her hat, she ran her fingers through her heavy dark locks and started to unbutton her jacket.

When she came to her boots, she could not see, so she went and retrieved the lamp and placed it on the floor.

The buttons on her boots were difficult to undo and she struggled, wishing that she had a boot hook.

"Oh, bother!" she exclaimed in frustration, as she snapped a fingernail.

Finally she managed to pull off her boots and began to roll down her stockings. Flinging them onto a chair, she bent down to pick up the lamp.

As she raised it, she happened to look towards the door and there, lolling in the doorway, was the figure of a man who was staring intently at her.

She almost jumped right out of her skin and then, with horror, she realised that he must have been watching her as she took off her garments.

"Who – just who are you?" she stammered, as she moved the lamp to get a better look.

The man's black hair fell over his face and he wore no jacket. His shirt was undone almost to the waist and in his hand he carried an open bottle of wine.

"A very pretty show!" he slurred in a heavy voice. "Now what have we here?"

Robina was frozen to the spot in horror as the man crossed the room to where she was standing.

As she tried to make out his face, she realised there was something vaguely familiar about his angled nose and wide lascivious mouth.

Something about the way his hair fell forward and his lip curled –

"Who, who are you? *Do* answer me," she repeated, her voice rising in panic.

Should she scream? Should she run?

A thousand thoughts teemed in her head as she was paralysed by fear.

The man lurched across the room and grabbed her wrist.

"Why, if it isn't little Robina Melville!" he snorted. "Except that you are not so little any more!"

He laughed and the sound filled her with terror.

She tried to pull herself free, but he was too strong.

Pulling her close to him, she could smell stale drink on his breath and heard his heavy breathing.

"And just why are you wandering around the castle at this hour? In fact, what are you doing here at all?"

She swung the lamp round and then she saw who her captor was.

"*Ellis*! Let go of me!" she shouted, hoping that she might be heard.

He pulled her closer so that she almost dropped the lamp.

She felt herself pressed against his damp chest and it revolted her to her very core.

"Let go of me, please," she whimpered, hoping that pleading with him would work.

"Not until you tell me why you are here," he said, "and besides, I think it's time we re-acquainted ourselves, don't you?"

He tried to kiss her, but she pulled away from him.

In the struggle the lamp smashed to the ground and the wind blew out the wick seconds before it hit the floor.

They were now both in total darkness.

Ellis renewed his grip and she battered him with her fists as he moved his face towards hers menacingly.

"You always were a high and mighty little miss," he grated, holding her so fast that she could neither move nor breathe. "And now you are going to be nice to me – "

Robina closed her eyes and opened her mouth to scream, while behind her the French doors banged noisily in the wind.

CHAPTER SIX

Robina closed her eyes and clamped her lips shut.

"Please, Ellis, don't!" she shouted, twisting her face away.

But Ellis only laughed – a low horrible laugh full of menace.

Suddenly from behind her came a full-blooded yell.

"Ellis! What on earth are you doing? Let go of her at once!"

"*Robert*!" cried out Robina, too terrified to consider that she had addressed him in a rather familiar fashion.

Pushing her away with a dismissive gesture, Ellis now let out a cruel laugh. She had heard that sound before when, as a child, he had pulled the legs off insects.

Robina fell to the ground and cut her hand on some fragments of glass from the smashed oil lamp.

"Now, get out of here," bawled the Earl to Ellis, in a cold voice that chilled Robina's blood. "I will deal with you later!"

As Ellis slunk out of the room, the Earl rushed over to where she was nursing her cut hand.

Tenderly brushing back her hair, he held her for a fleeting moment.

"Are you all right?" he asked very gently.

He was staring into her face with a concerned air.

"My hand is bleeding – oh, Robert."

He took a large handkerchief from the pocket of his dressing gown and deftly wound it around her hand.

"Ssh, you are safe now. I will ring for Mrs. Osidge to take care of you. I am certain that all this rumpus has awoken her."

"I am so so terribly sorry!" she sobbed, holding the handkerchief firmly around her hand. "I had to get away from home and you said that I was always welcome here."

"What can have happened to make you run away in the middle of the night?"

"My Stepmama drove me to it. The man she invited to dinner was horrid! Old, fat and disgusting and the way he looked at me made me feel sick. His eyes raked over me as if I was only wearing my under-garments!"

"And was the subject of marriage raised?"

"I believe so. At the end of dinner he disappeared off with Papa for a talk and then, I was summoned into the drawing room and told he would be taking me for a drive the next day. I assume he intended to propose – why else would he seek to get me on my own?"

He did not like to say what was in his head, but he feared the worst.

Robina continued,

"And so, I decided to run away. I thought that if I was not at home when he arrived for me, then perhaps, he might go away. I did not think that I would go from one peril straight into another!"

The Earl sighed deeply.

"Ellis suddenly appeared not so long after you left yesterday. There has been trouble with one of the girls at the *Gaiety Theatre* – a matter of some delicacy that is not fit for your ears.

"Suffice it to say Ellis is in hiding and so, like you,

sought refuge at the castle. He had not been here for five minutes before he began to drink the contents of my cellar. I am afraid he is rather inebriated – that was his third bottle of claret you saw him with."

"So he has run away to escape the consequences of his actions? Then he is not a man!" cried Robina.

"I agree with you. The worst thing is that Ellis has heaped shame on the Hampton name with his deeds. I will have to keep him closely in check and cut off his allowance properly this time."

"I thought you had already done so."

"I said I would, but then I relented and gave him a small monthly sum. I can see that the only way forward is to keep him on a tight rein."

Just at that very moment, Mrs. Osidge appeared in a mobcap and wearing a green dressing gown. In her hand, was an oil lamp.

"My Lord, I thought I could hear a woman crying out and so I came to investigate. The kitchen door is wide open, has that brother of yours been prowling round again? We heard that he had returned to the castle – "

"It is well that you are here as I was on the point of ringing for you. Mrs. Osidge, Miss Melville has hurt her hand. Could you have this mess cleared up and a bandage brought for her?"

"I shall do it myself, my Lord,"

She disappeared off down the dark corridor.

The Earl sighed once more.

"Even the servants know of my brother's character and are on their guard."

"He frightened me so much – I was *so* terrified that he would do something untoward."

"Ellis may well be cruel, but he is not stupid. Your

father is a gentleman to be reckoned with and I would not have cared to have been in Ellis's shoes had he gone any further. No, I believe his sole intention was to frighten you – it has always been that way with him."

"How can two brothers be so utterly unalike?"

The Earl smiled.

"Look, here is Mrs. Osidge. She will take care of you and make you comfortable. Anything you wish for, just ask. Now, I must return to my bed and I will see you at breakfast tomorrow. Good night, Robina."

Mrs. Osidge fussed and tended to Robina's wound.

"There you go, miss. You were so lucky it was not deep. You get into bed and I will bring you some hot milk and I will ask Jessie to wake you at ten. I am certain that his Lordship will not be expecting you to start work at nine o'clock on the dot."

Robina quickly changed into her night clothes and jumped into bed.

She drank all the milk that Mrs. Osidge had brought and fell into a deep sleep.

*

The next morning, as she was awakened by Jessie pulling the curtains, for a moment, she did not know where she was.

And then she remembered the events of last night.

"His Lordship says he will be pleased to see you in the dining room in half an hour, miss."

"Thank you, Jessie."

She stayed in bed for a while thinking about what the day might bring.

Looking at the clock and seeing that it was ten past ten, she wondered what would happen when Lord Drury would soon arrive at Trentham House to find her not there.

'Stepmama will be furious! She will believe I have gone out riding. I am sure she will check the stables first to see if Firefly is there.'

She dressed herself and by half-past ten, was sitting downstairs in the empty dining room waiting for the Earl to arrive.

'I do hope that Ellis will not be eating with us,' she worried, as she heard footsteps on the stairs.

To her immense relief it was the Earl who entered the room, a broad smile on his face.

"I trust you managed to sleep a little?" he asked, as he sat down at the head of the table.

"Yes, I did, thank you. I was so tired that nothing could have awakened me."

"I am glad, but I do sense that you are still a little nervous. You must not concern yourself – Ellis will not be having breakfast as he is very busy sleeping off those three bottles of claret he drank last night!"

Robina managed to laugh.

"I cannot apologise to you enough for my brother. It appears it is not enough that he has already compromised the virtue of one girl, but he must then assault another!"

"It did seem to me as if I was in the midst of some long and terrifying nightmare," she confessed. "First, Lord Drury and then Ellis!"

"I expect, as we speak, that Lord Drury is hopping up and down in his carriage, furious you are not at home."

Robina smiled, but her broad smile belied the fear that every time she heard a noise in the hall, she expected it to be her stepmother, waiting to drag her off back home.

"Do you think you will be feeling well enough to work this morning?" asked the Earl.

"Of course. We may be a little late in starting our

tasks ahead, but I am looking forward to immersing myself in them. I wish only to erase the memory of last night."

"That might be impossible as Ellis is staying at the castle. However, I shall endeavour to see that he does not trouble you any further. Although, as you are such a pretty girl, I cannot fault his taste on this occasion!"

Blushing deeply, Robina cast down her eyes.

"Thank you," she replied, feeling embarrassed yet pleased that the Earl thought her attractive.

They finished their breakfast and then proceeded to the study. There was still so much to do and Robina's first task was to finish answering the Earl's letters.

They both worked in silence until the clock in the hall struck half-past twelve.

The Earl looked up from his plans and stretched.

"Do you think it might be an idea if you opened up the Tower to the public?" asked Robina, as she stacked up the pile of replies she had tackled that morning.

"Do you believe that people might find it amusing to climb so many stairs?"

"No, but the views from the top are so spectacular. I have often thought they are among the finest in the whole of England. I believe that if you made it the highlight of the tour, people would come from far and wide."

"With large cups of tea after they have made their assent, I assume?"

Robina chuckled.

"Now you are teasing me. Of course, we must give them something after their exertions. I would suggest tea with homemade scones, jam and clotted cream, cucumber sandwiches and assorted cakes. You could serve it in the garden, if the weather is fine."

"And if it rains?"

"Then we should retire to the Summer House."

"I am afraid that the Summer House is in dire need of repair. To be honest, I was thinking of demolishing it and building an Orangery."

"Even better!" cried Robina, jumping up from her chair. "I have often thought that one would look wonderful set amongst the gardens that back onto the East wing."

"Then, that is what I shall do. Really, Robina, you have the most wonderfully inventive ideas. I do not know what I would do without you. I just adore the Continental flavour that you bring to everything."

"The Lamonts found me a most willing pupil when it came to instructing me in the French way of life. Tell me, my Lord, have you thought of installing a large piece of modern sculpture in the grounds? Monsieur Rodin has many such pieces in his workshop that are for sale."

"And should I travel over to Paris to view them?" asked the Earl with a mock-serious air.

"I would be happy to undertake such a journey on your behalf," answered Robina, thrilled that she might, at last, be able to view the artist's studio.

Next Marriott came in to ask when they would care for luncheon.

"Goodness, is it time to eat again already?" laughed Robina, who had lost all track of the hours since she had entered the study.

"Luncheon will be a little late today, miss."

"And it would appear that your dreaded stepmother has not yet come crashing into Hampton Castle as you had feared," added the Earl.

"Yes, but I am wondering if Papa is concerned by my absence. We have grown so apart since my return. He seems preoccupied with my Stepmama. For instance, it is the anniversary of Mama's death this Saturday and when I visited the local florist, she said that he had yet to put in his order for flowers."

"I am certain it is the case that your father is simply overwhelmed by the building works that are happening at your home."

"I do hope so, as he has not said a word to me about the arrangements for visiting her grave and there is so little time now."

As they continued their work, Robina had an awful feeling that he had forgotten all about it.

'Much as I don't wish to return home, this evening, I must,' she decided with her heart sinking at the thought.

*

The afternoon sped past as quickly as the morning had done.

Neither the Earl nor Robina stopped to take the tea brought in by Marriott at four o'clock and so it stood on the side table growing cold.

As it grew ever later, Robina kept one eye upon the clock, knowing she would have to take her leave before it got too late.

"Will you be staying for dinner tonight?" asked the Earl hopefully, as the clock struck half-past five.

"No, I am afraid I must return home and face up to whatever is thrown at me. But thank you for the offer."

"You must think of this as your second home," said the Earl, rising to ring for Marriott to request that Firefly be made ready for Robina.

"I am grateful for your kind offer, but really, I shall be quite all right. If I do not return in the morning, though, then promise me that you will send a carriage for me."

"Do you really think that your stepmother will try to

keep you at the house against your will?"

"With her stubbornness, there is no knowing what she might do. Stepmama is accustomed to getting her own way and considering the feelings of others appears to mean little to her. She will want to put her foot down firmly with me over the matter of Lord Drury."

"But she cannot force you to marry him?"

"She will do her best. It is in her interests that I am removed from home as soon as possible. I also cannot rule out the possibility that she will send me packing back to France."

"Surely, your father will not allow that?"

"Papa seems to bend to the will of Stepmama these days," answered Robina with a sigh. "He cares not for my feelings or desires."

"I just cannot believe it," remarked the Earl, putting away his papers and plans.

"I would not have believed it had it not happened to me," answered Robina sadly.

She was thinking of the impending anniversary.

There was a silence as she tidied her desk.

As she did so, she could feel the Earl's eyes on her and something made her wary of looking up.

His stare unnerved yet excited her at the same time.

She could tell that he was appreciating her beauty rather than her efficiency.

'It is very flattering that he thinks I am attractive, but I must remind myself that he is my employer and thus it is impossible for there to be anything at all between us. Besides, I am resolute in my desire to remain unmarried for as long as possible.'

Outside, the Earl lingered as she mounted Firefly, who had been well rested and was champing at the bit to gallop over the fields.

"See how he longs to stretch his legs," said Robina, laughing at her feisty mount.

"He is a truly free-spirited animal," agreed the Earl. "It is a pity that I must stay at the castle, otherwise I would accompany you back home on Jet. You will not have met him – he is as black as night and would give your Firefly some stiff competition."

"One of these days, I shall challenge you to a race!" exclaimed Robina. "But for today, I must return home."

"Are you certain that you cannot stay tonight?" he enquired once more.

Robina sighed deeply as she would have loved to have stayed and not face the wrath of her stepmother, but she knew that it would only make matters much worse.

"No, thank you so much. I must return home and see that my Papa has ordered his flowers, but I will see you tomorrow morning, as usual. I am leaving my bags here, just in case I should need to flee at any time in the future!"

"Thank you so much for such a good day's work, Robina. The pleasure has been all mine."

The Earl had such a sad look on his face that she almost relented.

There was something in his eyes that told her that his interest in her was more than that of someone who was just a friend.

She waved one last time and set off down the drive.

'I must be as calm as I can to face Stepmama,' she told herself, as Firefly raced home across the fields.

*

By the time she arrived home, Robina was tired.

She was greeted by Newman who informed her that dinner was about to be served.

'Oh dear. I am still in my riding habit. No matter –

I won't run the risk of another telling-off for being late.'

Handing Newman her hat and gloves, she walked to the mirror on the wall and adjusted her hair.

She was flushed from her riding and her eyes shone – Robina was never happier than when she was on a horse.

Taking a deep breath, she entered the dining room.

As usual her stepmother was dressed rather richly and the diamonds around her throat sparkled brilliantly.

'Those look as if they are Mama's,' she thought, as she silently took her seat. 'Surely Papa has not given them to *her*?'

"I am sorry for being a little late," she murmured, as she sank down into the velvet-upholstered chair.

"We shall speak about your absence after we have finished dinner," her father began sternly. "I don't wish to ruin my appetite for the time being."

Her stepmother glared at her.

"It is a fine thing to have a daughter who cares so little about her father's feelings that she embarrasses him without any hesitation," she fumed.

"Laura, we will speak of this after we have eaten," her repeated firmly.

"Herbert, if you are willing to indulge the girl when she has been so abominably rude and selfish, then I am not. I didn't know what to say to Lord Drury when he arrived this morning to find that she was not at home."

"But Stepmama, I told you that I was expected at the castle. If Lord Drury had been so interested to see me, then he could have driven over there to collect me!"

"Don't be impertinent, Robina. Laura is absolutely right. You have embarrassed all of us with your behaviour. Now, enough of this – Newman, please serve the soup."

Robina felt stung by her father's words.

Surely he understood why she had run off, but she was glad he did not know she had taken off in the middle of the night.

'And at least I know I can trust the stable boys,' she thought, as she dipped her spoon into the crayfish soup.

The meal passed in silence with Robina anxious at what her stepmother was going to say to her next.

The moment that the dessert had been taken away, Laura rounded on her.

"You are the rudest and most ungrateful girl I have ever met!" she spat. "Lord Drury is so highly eligible and now, you have more than likely ruined your chances with him. Do you think that gentlemen such as he drop out of the trees every day? You are stupid and unruly."

"Your behaviour is just reprehensible," added her father. "A Melville's word is their bond and you agreed to ride out with Lord Drury, so why were you not here this morning?"

Robina felt crushed. Hot tears sprang into her eyes and it was all she could do to control herself.

"But Papa, I had told you that I was expected at the castle."

"Laura went to a great deal of trouble to introduce you to him and he was sufficiently interested in you to ask if I would have any objection to him paying court to you with a view to marriage."

"Papa, I don't wish to marry anyone at present – be it Lord Drury or the Prince of Wales, himself! I am happy as I am. Besides I have only recently returned home and I wish to spend time with you."

"What you wish for yourself is immaterial," chimed in Laura, "we are not here to dance attendance on you! If your father and I wish you to marry, then marry you will! Is that understood?

"And as for this foolish notion about employment – your new husband, whoever he is, will not want a wife who works. It seems to me there is no alternative. We should send you back to France on the very next boat."

Robina felt like responding to this barrage, but her father interrupted.

"Laura, have you forgotten the reason I asked her to return from France in the first place? Has it slipped your mind, perhaps, that it is now the anniversary of Robina's mother's death this very weekend?"

"Oh, I am sorry," she replied awkwardly, realising that she had just committed a dreadful error of judgement in pushing the matter too far.

"No, Robina must remain at least until the weekend and then I will make a decision. I am her father, Laura, and the only one to decide her fate – not you! Robina, we shall not speak of this again until after the weekend."

She was stunned at his apparent change in attitude.

"Yes, Papa," Robina answered meekly, yet secretly she was thrilled that he had, in her eyes, stood up for her.

'Maybe he has changed his mind on marrying me off,' she thought, as they rose to retire to the drawing room for coffee. 'Perhaps he has decided that my place is with him after all.'

Robina did not stay up very long.

She felt in need of a long hot bath after her ride and now, pleasantly full, she took her leave and retired.

Just as she was leaving, her father spoke to her,

"Robina, I have ordered flowers for the grave and I trust that the Earl will not be requiring you on Saturday?"

"No, Papa."

"Very well, we shall leave for the churchyard after breakfast."

Robina was ecstatic.

'I was wrong to believe Papa would forget all about Saturday,' she thought, as she climbed upstairs.

After a delicious bath she was about to settle herself down for the night when there was a loud knocking at her bedroom door.

'How strange,' she thought, as she hurriedly put on her dressing-gown.

She expected it to be Molly, grumbling that she had forgotten something, so she was surprised to see Newman standing there holding a salver in his hand.

"I am so sorry to disturb you, miss, but this has just been delivered by hand."

"Really? Who brought it?"

"It was a messenger on horseback, miss. I believe it is from the castle. Look – that is the Hampton crest."

Robina turned the letter over and looked at the red-wax seal.

It was, as Newman had guessed, the Earl's crest.

Eagerly tearing open the letter, she began to read,

"*My dear Robina,*" it said.

"*I do hope that your evening has passed off without event. I am writing to request that you do not come to the castle tomorrow as planned, or indeed, next week either.*

I cannot say why, but I would ask you to await my further instructions.

I will write to you again in due course when I have need of your services.

Yours, Robert Hampton."

"Oh!" she cried out loud.

She got back into bed, feeling heavy of heart.

'What has occurred to make him change his mind?' she wondered, as she stared up at the ceiling. 'Is Ellis in trouble again and the Earl has been forced to sort out the matter?'

The more she ruminated about it, the more worried she became.

'Has he been taken ill or perhaps a relative has died and he has only just received the news?'

Even though she was feeling exhausted, all manner of thoughts persisted in crowding into her mind.

And the last picture she could see before she drifted off to a deep sleep was of the Earl's handsome face – his bright blue eyes burning with simmering emotion.

CHAPTER SEVEN

But the Earl did not send for Robina the next day, or the day after that.

If it had not have been for her growing sense of uneasiness, she might well not have worried quite so much that she had somehow either caused him offence or he had decided that he no longer required her services.

Laura did not make life any easier for her either by following Robina wherever she went.

'Must she keep such a close eye on me?' thought Robina angrily, as she spied her standing on the terrace, looking down the garden, while she sat by the fountain.

It had become one of her favourite places to sit and think and, now, her stepmother was making it very difficult for her to relax.

'I hope that she is not about to come and give me yet another lecture about Lord Drury,' she muttered, as her stepmother came walking towards her.

"Robina!"

"Yes, Stepmama."

"I have had a letter from Lord Drury. You are most fortunate as he is prepared to forgive your bad manners and has expressed an interest in visiting us for dinner again. As it is your mother's anniversary this weekend, I shall leave it until next week before I invite him again."

"Very well, Stepmama."

"And have I your promise that this time, you will be cooperative?"

Robina hung her head – she had no wish to see the man ever again, but she also did not wish to tell a lie.

"I will be present at dinner," she responded, after a long pause. "I promise you."

Laura appeared satisfied with her assurance and left without another word.

'Am I to be hounded by her for desiring a choice in this matter?' mused Robina, as she dropped her hand into the cool water. 'Oh, Mama! I wish you had not died! You would not have forced me to marry against my will.'

Robina knew that she was utterly powerless.

As her father seemed uninterested in her feelings, there really was nothing she could do.

'If I go against him, then I will risk losing his love altogether. I want to be a dutiful daughter, but how can I when that path leads to utter misery for me? If I was his son, would he be seeking to force me into marriage?'

But if she had been a son, perhaps Robina would not have had the same struggle with her stepmother for she would not have been considered as a rival for her father's affections.

'Such is the lot of mere women,' she reflected and, not for the first time, she wished she had been born a boy.

Robina stayed by the fountain for some time, lost in thought.

She did not see her stepmother going out in the new brougham.

*

Later she decided to write to Hortense Lamont.

She went up to her bedroom, pulled out a sheet of paper from the drawer and began to write in French.

In the letter, she asked if she could come and stay indefinitely, should her situation not improve.

'There, it is done! If necessary, I will voluntarily remove myself to France. I shall take Nanny with me and we shall find ourselves a small apartment to live in.'

Nanny. Where is she?

Robina realised that she had not seen Nanny for a couple of days.

She rang for Molly and asked her,

"Molly, where is Nanny? Is she ill?"

"I don't know where she is, miss."

"Would you go and find her, please? I wish her to keep me company."

The girl looked confused and Robina suddenly felt fear gripping her heart.

"Is Nanny well? Has something happened?"

"No, miss," muttered Molly, "I will go to find her."

"Thank you," answered Robina, a little unnerved by their discourse.

But Nanny did not appear and Molly returned with some excuse about Nanny having to go back to the village for a while.

And there was still the letter to Hortense to post.

She could not possibly trust Molly with the task, so she decided to take the letter to the Post Office herself.

She put on her hat and gloves and ran downstairs.

'I'll ask Charles to make the new brougham ready,' she thought, as she walked towards the stables.

The courtyard was a hive of activity as usual.

Jack was busy with a barrow of straw, while Charles was supervising the grooming of her stepmother's horse.

"Good morning, miss," he called and waved.

"So, has my stepmother taken poor Pearl for a ride, yet?"

"No, miss. We're about to put her out to the field so she can have a gallop. It's a shame as she's a sociable horse and likes us humans."

"Perhaps I should take her out. Tell me, Charles, can she pull the brougham?"

"Not really, miss. She's not really suited to it. But she be a fine mount for a lady."

Robina stroked the dapple-grey mare fondly.

"If you're wanting to go out today, miss, why don't you take her? The Mistress won't notice."

"I had come to ask for the brougham – "

"Oh, it won't be possible, miss. The Mistress took it out earlier."

"Oh, she did not mention she was going out when I saw her earlier."

"Gone into the town, no doubt," suggested Charles, picking up a bridle. "Shall I get the phaeton ready for you instead?"

"No, saddle up Pearl. She shall not linger unloved in her stall any longer."

"Right you are, miss. She'll be thrilled to be taken out good and proper like."

Robina felt a delicious sense of wickedness. If her stepmother refused to exercise her horse, then she would.

"I hope Firefly will not be too jealous!"

"Oh, don't you worry about him, miss. He's out in the field with Peony and Hercules. They're busy eating the clover and chasing each other."

Robina laughed.

She jumped up on the box and mounted Pearl. She could sense that the mare was excited at the prospect of a ride out.

"There's a good girl," crooned Robina, patting her neck. "Come on, we shall let you stretch your legs."

Very soon she was galloping down the drive. Pearl was not as solid as Firefly, but she had a sure step and was surprisingly swift.

Robina took her across the fields and up to a small wood on the outskirts of the village.

Pearl plunged through the green canopy without a second thought and Robina laughed out in delight as they passed through the forest.

"It's a pity Stepmama does not take you out more often. You are a brave little horse."

Remembering her letter Robina turned Pearl around and headed towards the village.

On the way she passed by *The Three Oaks Inn* and saw, to her utter amazement, the new brougham standing outside.

'How peculiar! Why is Stepmama visiting the inn?'

However, she did not linger in case her stepmother appeared and saw her, so she urged Pearl on and they rode into the village.

She posted the letter and even though a part of her wanted to ride past the inn again, she refrained from doing so.

'My Stepmama is up to something, but I dare not confront her about it. I shall have to find out through some other means.'

By the time she returned, all manner of theories had occurred to her.

'Was Stepmama meeting Lord Drury at the inn or was it some another man? If she is deceiving Papa, then I must endeavour to uncover evidence of it. Surely he

93

would send her packing if he found her to be unfaithful to him?'

Much as she realised it would hurt him, she secretly wished her stepmother's virtue to be questionable – would that not make things a great deal easier for her?

She returned Pearl to the stables and as she slipped in through the French windows, she heard her stepmother's voice in the hall.

'So, she is back,' thought Robina, as she stood in the shadows in the corridor by the stairs.

"Newman, please don't allow anyone to disturb me, I am going to take a nap once I have taken luncheon in my room," she heard her say.

'Perhaps I shall have a chance to speak with Papa,' Robina told herself, as she emerged from the corridor.

The dining room was ready for luncheon.

"Good afternoon, miss," Newman now greeted her brightly as she entered.

"What is for luncheon?" she asked in anticipation as the long ride had made her feel hungry.

"Cold chicken and a selection of vegetables."

"And for pudding?"

"A peach tart, miss."

Robina sat down and gleefully awaited her father's entrance.

She did not have to wait for long as he entered the room a few moments later.

"Ah, Robina!" he exclaimed, his eyes lighting up. "I am so pleased that you and I will have the opportunity to talk. Laura is a little tired after a morning of charity work in the village. I think it depresses her to see such poverty."

Robina was quite taken aback.

She could not see her undertaking any charity work in *The Three Oaks Inn*!

"Did she say what she was doing, precisely? I often find myself with time upon my hands and perhaps I could join her," she said carefully.

"Oh, I think it is tending the sick and looking after the children whose parents are forced to leave them so that they can go out and earn money."

"I did not realise that there were so many waifs and strays in the village."

"'*If you look, so ye shall find*' – is that not what the Bible taught us?"

Robina merely smiled in reply.

So her stepmother was not being truthful!

Even if her father believed this stuff about feeding stray children, she did not! There was indeed a charity for the poor run by the Church, but usually the helpers visited nearby villages.

"I have ordered my floral tribute for your Mama's grave," said her father suddenly, "it is being delivered this afternoon along with your own."

"When shall we visit the cemetery?"

"I have ordered the phaeton to be ready for us after breakfast. Laura will not be coming with us as I told her it would not be necessary."

Robina smiled at him gratefully.

"I have asked the Vicar to attend us and say a few words. It will be a simple reading and a blessing."

Robina reached out across the table and touched her father's hand.

"Thank you, Papa," she said in a low tearful voice. "That is a wonderful thing to do. I am certain that if Mama is up in Heaven looking down on us, she would be pleased to be remembered in this way."

He allowed Robina's hand to rest on his for a few moments.

'Papa does still love me. And Mama too,' thought Robina, blinking back her tears.

She felt a strong surge of emotion as they sat there and finished their meal together.

They talked about the house and the renovation and then he asked her about the Earl.

"Have you relinquished your post at the castle?" he asked, as the peach tart was served.

"No, Papa, but there is a family problem that he has to resolve and so I am not required for a few days."

"Ellis?"

"Yes, I believe so."

"I count myself most fortunate that I do not have a wayward son such as he, but I am still concerned over this matter of your attitude to Lord Drury."

Robina flushed red with embarrassment.

Upsetting her stepmother was one thing – but how she hated Papa to be angry with her.

"I am so sorry, Papa, but I cannot marry a man I do not love."

"Love may grow, Robina. I know he is not in the first flush of youth, but he is a good man with considerable means. You would have a very comfortable life with him and I should not have to worry about you."

"But Papa, do you not wish me to be happy in the same way that you and Mama were?"

He looked fixedly into the far distance and avoided meeting her gaze.

She could see he was recalling all the sweet days he had spent with her Mama –

After a long pause he seemed to check himself and answered,

"You are too romantic, Robina. I have come to believe that it is much better to marry someone with whom you are not much in love, as, if anything should happen to them, it is a great deal easier to bear."

She was about to answer, when Newman entered and announced that Sir Herbert had a visitor.

"Ah, a little earlier than I had expected," he sighed, "will you please excuse me, my dear?"

Robina nodded and watched sadly as he left.

'Why does he deny me happiness in this way?' she thought, feeling terribly let down.

She had had such high hopes of persuading him to see things from her point of view and she had failed.

'It would seem that losing my Mama has made him so jaded towards the very notion of romance. I must resign myself to leaving for France in that case.'

*

Saturday morning dawned, fine and warm.

Robina put on full mourning and spent time looking at her mother's photograph before she went down to breakfast.

'A whole year without you, Mama,' she whispered, as she looked into her eyes. 'It does not seem possible.'

Downstairs her father was in a solemn mood. He barely acknowledged her as she entered the dining room.

Laura was nowhere to be seen.

"Where is Stepmama?" asked Robina, as she sank down into an armchair. The bombazine-crepe dress rustled as she made herself comfortable.

"She is out again – yet more charity work," said her father with an exasperated tone creeping into his voice.

"She must feel as if she is intruding on our grief, so I expect that is why she removed herself."

Her father did not reply.

Newman came in and Robina noticed that he was wearing a black armband over his jacket. She smiled at him and acknowledged this small show of thoughtfulness.

'Mama was very fond of Newman. She was a good judge of character and would be most touched to see him honouring her memory in this way.'

Immediately after breakfast, Newman came in and announced that the carriage was ready for them.

Robina donned a black cape and waited in the hall as Newman brought out the floral tributes from the kitchen.

"They have survived quite well, miss," he said in a quiet respectful voice, as he carried them to the carriage.

"Yes, they have," she agreed, gazing at the mound of white carnations that made up her father's tribute.

The arrangement she had chosen was a small posy of yellow roses – she had always given such a bouquet to her mother on her birthday.

The phaeton had been highly polished so that one could see one's face in its shiny black doors and Robina noticed that black had replaced the dark red curtains.

She climbed in and waited for her father to join her.

Her mother was buried in the local churchyard in an elegant tomb with four columns so as to resemble a Greek temple.

St. Matthew's Church was at the edge of the village and it was where Robina was christened and confirmed.

She had not felt able to face any of the services at

the Church since she had returned from France, as there were too many memories attached to the place.

As the phaeton pulled up at the Church, she hoped that the Vicar would not reprimand her for not attending his services.

She need not have worried too much, as he said a prayer, gave a blessing and then disappeared to leave them to their memories.

Robina marvelled at the fine carving of the tomb and the inscription that was simple yet poignant.

She laid her posy behind the railings and waited for her father to rest his wreath of carnations against it.

They stood for some moments in silence – Robina did not meet her father's eyes for she knew that she would see tears there.

She wanted to weep and wail as a wave of grief hit her, but she restrained herself.

She could not, however, prevent a single tear from coursing down her cheek.

'I do so wish I had a friend I could confide in,' she reflected, as they stood by the tomb.

She immediately thought of the Earl.

'I just wish he would summon me to the castle,' she pondered, as they made their way across the churchyard to where the phaeton was waiting for them.

As they pulled away, Robina took the opportunity to ask her father something that was troubling her.

"Papa," she began, hoping he would hear her out, "I am still finding it difficult to understand why you felt that you had to marry again so soon after Mama's death."

He sighed heavily as if he did no wish to answer the question, but after a while, he responded,

"I was so very lonely after your Mama died. It was as if my entire world had collapsed. She was everything to me and I found it so hard to cope without her. When Lady Wolverton appeared, it was as if your Mama had sent her from Heaven."

"But Papa, you had me! Surely if you had kept me at home, instead of sending me off to Paris, I could have comforted you?"

"Robina, you completely fail to understand, you are my daughter and I have need of a wife!"

She could not help herself – hot tears scalded down her cheeks.

"Furthermore, whilst we are on the subject, I would ask you to be more pleasant and amenable to Laura. She is a sensitive woman and she feels as if you are not accepting her. She only has your best interests at heart and I think it is very kind of her to search for a suitable match for you."

"But Papa – "

"No, Robina, I will not hear the same arguments again. You must promise me that when Lord Drury comes to dinner again you will be compliant with our wishes. You must at least let him call on you and pay you court. If you find him utterly disagreeable, then we will have to discuss the matter further at that point. If you love me, then you will do this small thing for me."

"Yes, Papa," answered Robina, feeling torn.

She did indeed love her Papa, but did it have to be at the expense of her own happiness?

"Good, I am glad that you have seen sense at last," he said with a satisfied air.

By the time they reached home, Robina was feeling very downhearted.

'Papa's love seems to be dependent upon me doing

as he says,' she thought, climbing down from the carriage. 'I cannot do anything that would jeopardise it.'

As they entered, Newman approached Robina.

"Excuse me, miss, but a letter has come for you."

"Is it from the Earl?" she asked eagerly.

"I believe so, miss. It bears his crest."

Her hands were shaking as she took the letter.

"Thank you, I will read it upstairs," she said, trying to control her sudden excitement.

Upstairs she closed the door firmly and took off her hat, gloves and cape.

She sat in her armchair and ripped open the letter.

"Dear Robina,

I am so sorry I have found it necessary to keep you away from the castle these past days. I am not at liberty to discuss the reasons at length in this letter – suffice to say that my brother plays a part in it.

I am also mindful of the fact that this weekend is the anniversary of your mother's death, but I would ask that you return to the castle at your earliest opportunity, as there is a matter of some delicacy that I would discuss with you.

Kind regards, Robert Hampton."

'Now here is a fine thing!' she mused. 'This letter poses more questions than it provides answers. I will make my way over to the castle first thing on Monday.'

She put the letter between the pages of a book and lay down on the bed for a while with her thoughts whirling.

'What can Ellis have done now? I had thought he had surpassed himself by attempting to assault me. I can only think that the young lady whom he compromised has put in an appearance – or perhaps, she is engaged and her fiancé has challenged Ellis to a duel!'

All kinds of wild ideas ran through her mind as she lay there.

'But it all is conjecture until I visit the Earl. I must wait until Monday to see what the mystery behind this very strange missive might be.'

In fact Monday could not come soon enough.

*

She felt grateful that the weekend passed peacefully enough. Her stepmother made no mention of Lord Drury and her father seemed almost affectionate towards her.

On Monday Robina decided to leave for the castle a bit later than usual and was glad that she did, for just after nine o'clock, a delivery man brought the new riding habit she had ordered just before she had left France.

As Molly brought in the box, Robina could not wait to open it. She dismissed the girl and eagerly cut the string.

Tearing off the lid and several layers of tissue paper she saw her new riding habit in a deep wine colour.

"Oh! It is so lovely," she gasped, as she shook the jacket from the box.

Running to the mirror, she pulled it on and admired her reflection. The dark colour suited her fair skin so well and made her brown eyes appear chestnut coloured.

The jacket fitted her perfectly and emphasised her slender figure. She held the skirt up to her body and saw that together the effect was stunning.

'I shall wear it today,' she decided, unhooking her skirt and slipping into the new one.

She hoped she would not be too warm in the jacket, but thankfully the weather was not as fine as last week.

Running downstairs in a great state of excitement, she completely forgot her riding gloves. She was halfway to the stables before she remembered them.

'Goodness. I cannot possibly ruin my hands again by not wearing them.'

She remembered the last time she had done so – the night she had flown Trentham House to avoid Lord Drury – and that she had given herself blisters that had only just healed up.

She turned back towards the house and ran upstairs.

She opened her bedroom door and was shocked to see that Molly was there, rummaging through her chest of drawers in a way that did not suggest she was rearranging them, but searching for something.

"Molly! What are you doing?"

She looked up and her mouth fell open in surprise.

"Oh, miss. I-I was looking for some mending."

"In my private drawers that you know you are not allowed to touch?" questioned Robina.

"I am sorry, miss. I must have forgotten."

"I think you had better leave the room, Molly. I am in a hurry so we shall speak of this later."

Molly hung her head and left the room.

Robina was furious.

'How dare she! She must have been put up to it by my stepmother.'

Robina found her gloves and went back downstairs, unsure as to what she should do.

She could reprimand the girl, for certain, but how could she now confront her stepmother? She had no firm evidence that it was she who was at the bottom of it all and she may say that as Mistress of the house, she was entitled to look there.

'I will have to deal with this matter later,' thought Robina, firmly, as she approached the stables.

As soon as she was riding Firefly, she forgot about Molly's sly behaviour and was looking forward to seeing the Earl once more.

On arrival at the castle she noticed that the builder's cart was parked at the side of the castle next to the Tower.

Men were mixing cement and carrying hods full of bricks up the winding stairs.

'Things are clearly well underway,' she thought, as she dismounted Firefly and walked towards the Earl who was standing at the base of the Tower in deep discussion with the foreman.

"Ah, Robina," he cried, with his eyes lighting up. "Can we meet by the stable field in fifteen minutes? I am certain that you will enjoy looking at my horses and I have a new Arab stallion I would very much like you to see."

"Oh, very well," replied Robina, a little taken aback that he had not asked her into the castle.

She wandered off towards the stables and found the Head Groom.

"His Lordship has told me that I may view his new acquisition."

"Aye, miss – come this way."

"This be Saladin," he said, indicating a handsome white stallion in the stall next to Firefly.

"My goodness. He is so beautiful!" cried Robina, putting her hand out to stroke the horse's nose.

"Better horse you won't find in the whole County," boasted the Head Groom before disappearing.

Robina admired the stallion for a few moments and then, having made sure that Firefly was not getting jealous, she made her way to the nearby field.

She enjoyed watching the horses running free and the Earl had a lush green field exclusively for their use.

She was entranced, watching the half dozen or so of the finest horses she had ever seen, as they gambolled and munched contentedly on bales of hay hanging from a tree.

'They are better cared for than some humans,' she thought.

A soft touch on her shoulder made her jump.

She turned around to find herself looking straight into the Earl's startlingly blue eyes.

"Robina, I do apologise for keeping you, but please come with me now, I wish to show you how the Tower is progressing."

He took her hand and Robina blushed to the very roots of her hair, as it was such an unexpected gesture.

She felt quite uncomfortable as he led her back to the Tower.

"Where are the men?" she asked, as they reached it.

"They are enjoying a tea break in the kitchen. Mrs. Osidge always has a large kettle on the hob in readiness for them. I am told they drink enough to water several fields!"

Robina laughed shyly for the Earl had yet to let go of her hand.

"Come, shall we climb up the Tower," he suggested gently as he looked into her eyes.

"But it is not yet finished – would you not prefer that I wait until it is?"

The Earl simply smiled back at her and led her into the dark entrance.

They climbed the winding stairs

'I wonder what it is that he wants to show me?' she reflected, as they reached the top, 'it is not as if I have not seen the view before.'

As they stood at the Tower's summit, she could see that some of the brickwork had been replaced and it would not be long before it was all restored to its former glory.

"Robina," began the Earl, taking her hand again, "I am sorry that I had to keep you away from the castle for a few days. There were several delicate matters to attend to that involved Ellis. You will not be seeing him again – I have sent him packing."

"Do you mean you have banished him?"

"I suppose you could say that, although banishing sounds rather drastic."

They both laughed and Robina caught something in his eyes that told her he had more to say.

"But that is not the reason I have asked you here," the Earl added.

Robina stayed silent, although inside her thoughts were far from still.

She felt nervous and uneasy.

"Robina," the Earl continued slowly, enfolding her hands with his hands. "I have been thinking of nothing but you for these past few days and I must tell you that I am utterly in love with you.

"That appalling business with Ellis has only served to compound what I was already feeling. If I am honest, I have loved you since we were children together and I am not a man to hold back when I have made my mind up, so I would be honoured if you will agree to be my *wife*."

Robina stood there with the wind blowing through her hair and the Earl holding onto her hands.

She looked into eyes that were so full of love that she could scarcely meet his gaze and did not know how to answer him.

"Please, Robina, what do you say to me?" he asked,

pleadingly, his blue eyes willing her to open up her heart to him.

A heart that at that very moment was wracked with confusion and astonishment.

CHAPTER EIGHT

The Earl gazed at Robina in expectation of a reply.

She could see in his eyes how much she meant to him.

'What shall I say to him that will not hurt him?' she thought, as the wind whipped at the loose ends of her hair. 'I am *not* ready for marriage.'

They stood there for several moments with Robina unable to reply and the Earl holding her hands tightly.

She could not meet his eyes for it pained her to see so much love there.

She felt confused – she liked him well enough, but *romance*?

At last he let go of her and said with a sad note in his voice,

"I can see that I have made a mistake in springing this on you. Forgive me and I will not mention it again as I have obviously spoken out of turn and it has embarrassed you. There are several letters that require attention, I will understand if you wish to go, but I would appreciate your help – matters have piled up over the past few days and I have not had the opportunity to attend to them. We will not speak of this matter again unless you wish to."

Robina felt very relieved but, at the same time, her heart and throat contracted with emotion.

'It is as if he has read my mind,' she thought.

She watched as his strong back moved down the staircase in front of her.

She could see that the workmen were in the process of installing electric lights as she had suggested.

'Goodness. I did not have the slightest notion that marriage could be on his mind,' she said to herself as they entered the study. 'I had no clue that he had ever thought of me romantically.'

The Earl rang for tea and they made a start at their day's work. What he had said was put to one side as they concentrated on clearing a mountain of correspondence.

Robina's efforts to entice tourists to the castle were beginning to pay off.

There was a long letter from a company in London which was interested in providing special carriages to ferry guests to the castle and another from a printer who offered generous discounts for invitations and leaflets.

"I have a letter here from Harrods who are happy to supply us with food in as large a quantity as we require," called out Robina enthusiastically.

"Well done, Robina," answered the Earl, giving her such a sad look that her heart almost melted. "Before we know it we shall have our first party of guests arriving and I do hope that we shall be ready in time."

"Might I suggest then that you start working on the decorating as soon as the rebuilding has been completed?"

The Earl paused for thought.

"In that case I need you to speak with the decorator at once. Things are progressing so fast that the first rooms will be finished before the end of the summer. I have not given any thought to colours – perhaps you can suggest some?"

"I would be delighted," replied Robina, "Mama had excellent taste and kept many samples at Trentham House. I shall write to her people in London and ask for samples of their latest ranges."

"Thank you. I confess I would not know where to start. I have always considered these kinds of things to be woman's territory."

"I would not expect an Army man to be conversant with the latest styles for the home," she parried, laughing, "in the same way that I would not have an idea how to lead a parade or plan a battle."

"Oh, you dignify my contribution too highly, I did not plan any battles in India. It was as much about keeping the peace as anything."

"But there is a skill in that too, I am certain. And you were responsible for a troop of men."

"Perhaps. But I am distinctly more scared by the thought of colour palettes than a whole host of marauding natives!"

As they laughed together, Robina was glad that any awkwardness between them had now disappeared.

But she did wonder why suddenly she seemed to be besieged by men who wanted to marry her!

'I am certain that there are many young ladies who would eagerly change places with me,' she mused, as she busied herself answering invitations to balls that the Earl had received and organising his diary, 'but marriage is not something I would want to consider at present.'

*

She worked tirelessly until five o'clock struck and then she yawned and stretched.

"Yes, I do believe it is time for you to go home," commented the Earl.

"But there is still much more to do," she protested, indicating a list of 'things to do' covering an entire page.

"I think you have done enough for one day, now, let me ring for Marriot to call for Firefly to be brought to the front for you."

"Thank you, I am just a little tired – " she confessed gratefully. "But before I leave today, there is something I wish to say to you."

"Oh?"

She took a deep breath.

"My Lord, I am very flattered by your proposal and I want you to realise that my refusal is not in any way a personal slight on you. You are a fine man and any woman would count herself fortunate to have you as a husband.

"However, I have no wish to marry anyone at all at present – in spite of what Papa and Stepmama would want – and I hope that we can remain friends and continue as we have been. I love working for you and I would not wish to jeopardise that."

The Earl looked down and slowly nodded his head to signify that he understood.

There was something about his manner that touched Robina's heart.

"But I have your assurance that our friendship will continue?" he asked without looking up.

"Of course," she replied, rising from the desk.

"Robina," said the Earl, "whatever you wish is my command. As I said this morning, we shall not speak of this again unless you desire it. Friends we are and friends we shall be."

'He really is such a gentleman,' she thought, as he accompanied her along the corridor to the front entrance.

*

Ten minutes later she was mounting Firefly and as she did so, she caught the Earl gazing at her wistfully.

"I shall see you again tomorrow morning at nine," she promised.

Racing off down the drive, she suddenly felt sad.

'Was I just a little hasty in refusing him? I do not understand why I have such a pain in my heart if I only feel friendship for him! I wish I had someone to advise me. It is at moments like this that I miss my Mama so much. She would know why it is that I feel like this.

'The Earl is a fine man and I would be most upset if he subsequently went off and courted another lady. After all when a man has marriage in mind – '

All the way back to Trentham House, Robina could not stop thinking about it.

She arrived home to find the phaeton was ready and waiting outside.

'Can my Stepmama be going away?' she wondered hopefully, as the footman brought out a large trunk.

Charles came up and helped her down from Firefly.

"Ah, look at him," he said fondly, "he be ready for his stall and a nice bucket of water!"

"Yes, we flew back today," she answered, patting the horse's big head. "Perhaps I should have named him Lightning!"

Charles laughed and then led the horse away.

At the very same moment her father appeared at the door, wearing one of his best suits and a top hat.

"Ah, Robina, I am glad that I have seen you before I depart. I have to leave for London and I shall be away for the next few days. I am sorry it is so sudden, but I must go as there are some problems in the office.

"One of my partners has died and all is in uproar. I cannot trust the young whippersnappers to run things and so I shall remain in London until we have sorted it all out.

"You will be fine here with Laura and I only ask that you remember the talk we had on Saturday and abide by your promise."

"Yes, Papa," she answered, as he climbed into the phaeton. "I wish you a pleasant journey."

She waved until the phaeton disappeared.

Walking back to the house, her first thought was of how she would now be alone with her stepmother.

It was not that she was frightened of her – more that she did not trust her. She had already shown that she could be vicious when her father was not present to protect her.

And then there was the business with Nanny.

In spite of repeated requests that Nanny attend her, she had not appeared. Even Newman did not seem certain as to the reason behind her returning to the village.

Robina had put it to the back of her mind till now, as for a while, she had believed that Nanny had wanted to return to her home, but with the prospect of there not being anyone to shield her from her stepmother's wrath, she was forced to reconsider her position.

Inside the house was very quiet save for the ticking of the hall clock.

'Hideous thing! How I hate it!' she mumbled.

She was well aware that each day a different article appeared in the house and took the place of something that her mother had chosen and loved.

Moving upstairs, she noticed that the portrait of her grandmother that was once at the top of the stairs had been moved. In its place was a rather clumsy still life of a fruit bowl and a trio of cats.

Robina wrinkled her nose at it – she did not care for cats, preferring horses and dogs. Cats were only useful for keeping rats down and she hoped that her stepmother was not about to bring the nasty creatures into the house!

No, just give her a fine horse – a proper animal – any day of the week.

Walking into her room, Robina quickly checked her drawers and the wardrobe for missing items, but everything appeared present and correct.

The room had been cleaned whilst she was out and it smelled of beeswax and carbolic.

Sighing, she took off her new riding habit and rang for Molly to collect it. It had become quite rumpled during her ride and needed pressing.

There was something about the way the girl would not meet her eye as she entered the room that made Robina suspicious.

She took the riding habit and was gone in a flash.

'I cannot bear the girl's insolence,' she thought, as she lay down on the bed for a rest before dinner.

She picked up her book from the bedside table and as she opened it, she was surprised to find that she could not find her place.

'I know I used the Earl's letter to mark the page,' she said to herself, 'and now I cannot remember where I was. Perhaps it fell out when I put the book back this morning.'

But search as she might, she did not find the letter.

Then the truth dawned on her.

"Molly!" she exclaimed out loud. "She must have taken it!"

A simmering fury swept over her. She snapped the book shut and was on the point of ringing for Molly when she heard a noise in the corridor outside.

Thinking that it might be Nanny returning, she ran and opened the door.

Emerging from Nanny's room were Newman and one of the footmen, carrying boxes of Nanny's belongings that had obviously all been packed up.

"Where are you going with those?"

Newman looked as if he wished he was invisible. The footman scuttled off with his box and left them alone.

"Newman, please, I need to know what is going on. I will not be angry with you as I am concerned for Nanny's well-being. If she is ill or something has happened to her, then I wish to know."

The butler put down the box and indicated with a gesture that they should speak softly.

"Miss Robina, Nanny has been dismissed. Did you not know? She has been informed that she is too old to be useful and has been sent back to her home. She cried and asked to see you, but her Ladyship would not permit it."

"*She* did this?" asked Robina, in a quavering voice.

She did not know whether to be angry or to cry.

"Yes, miss. Her Ladyship ordered it herself."

"And is Papa aware of this?"

"I did not ask. We do not question her Ladyship's orders or wishes."

Robina was utterly shocked.

'I would guess Papa knows nothing about this,' she thought to herself.

"Thank you, Newman."

He picked up the boxes he had been carrying and took them downstairs.

Robina walked slowly back to her room to think.

She simply must now confront her stepmother and as for her Nanny – she must believe she had been deserted.

'I have a responsibility for Nanny,' decided Robina, 'tomorrow, I shall go to the village after I have finished my duties at the castle and find her. She must feel so alone and unwanted.'

*

The gong sounded at eight o'clock on the dot.

Robina changed into the pale-lemon silk dress she had bought in Paris. She always felt very chic in it and, as she knew that her stepmother would not be dressing down, she did not wish to give her any cause to make remarks.

She felt somewhat nervous at the thought of dining alone with Laura.

Robina collected herself and walked downstairs.

The dining room door was open as she reached the last stair, so she took a deep breath and went inside.

Her stepmother was already seated at the table and threw Robina an impatient look as she entered the room.

"Good evening, Stepmama."

"On time for a change," she responded sourly. "To what do I owe this honour?"

Robina was not certain if she was posing a question or making a comment.

"I am very sorry, Stepmama, I have obviously done something to annoy you, but I cannot think what it is."

She sat down in her chair and waited for a reply.

Laura was yet again wearing her Mama's diamonds and Robina had to bite her lip so as not to make a remark.

To her surprise she simply laughed.

"Don't look so serious, Robina – do you not have any sense of humour? You must take after your mother as Herbert has the most delicious sense of fun!"

Robina wanted to shout that her Mama had the best sense of humour in the world and that they had laughed so much, but she could see Laura's attempt to irk her for what it was.

"Now," she continued, "I have a surprise for you. Lord Drury will be coming for dinner on Wednesday and I will expect no resistance this time. I believe your father has spoken with you on the subject?"

"Yes, Stepmama, he has."

"So, I can count on your cooperation this time?"

"As I have told both you and Papa, I will be there."

"Good. There is also another matter I would wish to discuss with you. I do not like the idea of your working for a living in the least. It is not fitting for the daughter of one of the most important gentlemen in the County to work as a common secretary – I want you to write to the Earl and tell him you cannot possibly continue to work for him."

"But, Stepmama, you misunderstand his intentions. He certainly does not see me as a *mere* secretary," replied Robina, who decided that it was high time that she threw her stepmother off course. "He has made it quite clear that he wishes to court me."

"Then why hasn't he asked to see your father? Any gentleman with intentions on a young lady would do. No, Robina, I do not believe you for a moment. In any case, the Earl is far too handsome and important to favour *you* with his attentions. Really, you are quite deluded."

"He declared his love for me only this morning, I do not tell lies. You can ask him *yourself*."

Her stepmother stared at her across the table with a mixture of loathing and disbelief. Her chest heaved and a slow flush of pink rose up it.

"Are you really asking me to believe this nonsense? If you think that by lying to me, you will be able to prevent Lord Drury wooing you, then you are very much mistaken. He is not a man to be easily deterred."

Robina could see that her trump card had fallen on fallow ground. What use was it if her stepmother totally refused to believe her? She could hardly go to the Earl and ask him to write a letter, stating that he had proposed to her and that she had turned him down!

Newman brought in a lobster bisque – usually one of Robina's favourites.

However, with her stepmother sitting there glaring at her, she found it difficult to consume anything.

They sat and ate in silence.

Finally, as the dessert was served, Robina found her tongue again.

"I was wondering where Nanny was," she asked, as casually as you could.

"I have dispensed with her services. She is too old to be of any further use and Molly is young and strong."

"I don't care for Molly," retorted Robina, "I would like Nanny back, please."

"Nanny has served this family for long enough. I am not concerned whether or not you like Molly, there is nothing wrong with her and so she will continue to be your maid."

Robina could see that she would not get the better of her stepmother by arguing. It was clear that she would not be swayed by any amount of pleading with her.

'Even if it means going behind everyone's back, I shall reinstate Nanny,' she vowed.

'I will never allow this – woman to drive a wedge between me and anyone from the past. I owe it to Mama's memory to ensure that one of her old servants is properly looked after and not just discarded because it suits my new Stepmama!'

With her mind made up, Robina's confidence grew.

She would bring Nanny back to Trentham House – she would!

CHAPTER NINE

To outward appearances, Robina appeared to be the compliant stepdaughter. That morning, over breakfast, she informed her stepmother she would tell the Earl that very day that she could no longer work for him.

"I shall explain it to him in person," said Robina, "I think that he deserves that much."

"That is so thoughtful of you, Robina," she replied with a triumphant smile, "and so you will be at the castle today?

"Do not mention that another is wooing you as it may offend him. If indeed he has proposed to you, as have you suggested, you must make quite certain that you do not upset him in any way as he is so important in this County. Your father would be most displeased if he came home to find he has been ostracised through your actions."

Robina was surprised that her stepmother appeared to be behaving in a more reasonable manner.

"Yes, I ought to stay for the day and finish off what I can. I promise I will not mention Lord Drury."

"Good. Make certain that he knows this is the last time you go there to work. I cannot imagine what he was thinking of employing you in the first instance! Could he not find some middle-class matron who would have done just as well?"

"I think it was my expertise in French that attracted his attention. He wishes to attract European visitors to the castle and my linguistic skills would have been useful."

"Oh, everyone speaks French these days," said her stepmother dismissively.

Robina could not help but smile, as she knew very well that Laura's French was poor.

She finished her breakfast and then made her way quickly to the stables where Firefly was waiting to take her to the castle.

'I don't like making false promises to anyone,' she thought as she galloped along, 'but if it means that I can do what I have to, then I am certain that God will forgive me.'

She arrived at the castle rapidly – it seemed that now Firefly knew the way so well he covered the distance incredibly speedily.

The Earl was outside the Tower as she arrived.

The builders were heaving the new battlements up the outside wall with a winch.

"Robina! Look over here," called the Earl. "The finishing touch. The men worked all night in order to be ready to install them this morning."

Robina nodded her head appreciatively.

With the Tower almost finished, she would have to concentrate on the interior decor rather sooner than she had thought.

"It will look magnificent," she said, as she jumped off Firefly and hurried over to where the Earl was standing.

He looked at her fondly as she drew level with him.

"There is something I wish to ask you," he began, confidentially. "I have just had the plans for the ballroom from the architect and I would like you to look at them and give me your opinion. Would you do that for me?"

"I would be delighted," answered Robina, thrilled that he trusted her judgement in consulting her.

The ballroom was originally two large rooms which the Earl intended to enlarge to create one huge space.

"I want it to be the finest ballroom in the whole of England," he enthused, as they reached the study. "But it has to be in full keeping with the style of the castle and it would not do to have anything too modern."

"Yes, I do agree, my Lord," remarked Robina, as she studied the plans. "These windows he has drawn, here and here – they are far too modern. They should be high and in the Tudor-style."

"That is what I thought too. But the architect is a frighteningly opinionated fellow and, to be truthful, I am a little in awe of him. If he was an Army man, I would know how to deal with him, but artistic types – "

Robina laughed.

"I understand what you are saying, but you must be firm. You are paying for these works and you must have what you want."

"Naturally. Now, Robina, there is something else I would have you do for me and I am afraid it involves your going out again."

He walked to the window and picked up a piece of panelling.

"Do you see this? It's a sample that the carpenter has sent me for the new library. I confess I am not fond of it, but I do not have the time to visit his workshop and see whatever else he has to offer.

"He is expecting me at eleven o'clock this morning, so I wondered if you would go in my stead? You may take my carriage."

"I would be happy to go," agreed Robina, getting up from her desk.

"Good, I will ask Marriott to have it made ready for

121

you. You will need to leave in about half an hour."

He had no idea that there was another reason why Robina would be thrilled to go into the village.

'I can see the carpenter and then ask the coachman to take me to Nanny's house,' she planned, almost rubbing her hands together in glee.

She hummed to herself as she worked.

Once or twice she looked up to find the Earl staring at her, but he immediately averted his eyes.

"Have you heard again from Ellis?" she enquired, as he looked down once more.

"Not a word. Not even a begging letter for money! Marriott said that he has heard he is staying in an inn in the village, but that no one has yet seen him. In any case, I am certain that wherever he is, the first I shall know is when I receive the bill!"

Robina hoped that she would never see Ellis again, although she felt it probable that he might rear his head at some point.

'Hopefully, I will not be around to witness it,' she thought, as Marriott announced that the carriage was ready.

"You should go now, Robina," suggested the Earl, putting down his pen.

"Do not wait for me to start luncheon," she said, as she left. "I often lose track of time when I am involved in choosing things."

"Very well, I will ask Mrs. Osidge to prepare a cold plate for when you return."

Robina felt a little sly, but she did not want anyone to know what she was up to.

Although she thought that the Earl probably would not mind her borrowing his carriage to see Nanny, she did not want to have to explain herself.

Outside Morton, the coachman, was waiting to open the door for her. The Earl's carriage bore his crest and was very smart indeed. It was dark green and the interior seats were dark-green velvet.

Robina sank into the plush seats and marvelled at the luxuriousness of the interior. It was far nicer than her father's newly refurbished phaeton.

'If only Stepmama could see me now,' she mused, smiling to herself, as the Earl's carriage pulled away from the castle and headed off for the village.

*

The carpenter's workshop was next to the smithy.

Robina knew it well as she had often accompanied Charles to buy supplies for their modest forge at Trentham House. There were some things that Charles could not do and, then, he would take the horse or the broken implement to Mr. Walters, the blacksmith.

Mr. Armstrong, the carpenter, was understandably surprised to see Robina alighting from the carriage and not the Earl.

"Why, Miss Melville. This is a pleasant surprise."

"I am the Earl's secretary now," Robina told him, shaking his hand, "and he has sent me to discuss the wood panelling with you."

Morton interrupted them.

"I'll take the carriage round to the rear and wait for you there, miss."

"Thank you so much, Morton," she replied, paying little heed to him.

She was far too excited at the prospect of choosing new wood panelling for the library.

Inside the carpenter's workshop, Robina inhaled the smell of sawdust and timber. It was almost as intoxicating as a visit to the florists and she loved the scent of freshly milled timber.

Mr. Armstrong employed two men and they shared a huge bench covered in sawdust and wood shavings.

"If you'd come over here, miss, I have the samples his Lordship is interested in."

Robina carefully studied the timber panels and then decided upon a light oak.

"Can this be waxed?" she asked.

"Of course. We will install it in its natural state as you see it here and then the French polisher can come in and finish it off."

"And is this extra?"

The carpenter looked thoughtful for a moment and then said,

"I'll include it, seeing as it's for the Earl."

Robina rewarded him with a beaming smile.

"Would you be good enough to let me take a panel away, so that I may show him what I have chosen? Here are the measurements for the library. I am certain that you will be able to work out how much is required from them."

"Very good, miss. Please do send his Lordship my best wishes," said Mr. Armstrong, as he escorted her to the rear of the workshop.

Morton was already in his box when she returned to the carpenter's yard and the carriage door was open.

'He is in a real hurry,' she thought as she climbed inside. 'I do hope he is not going to be too grumpy that I now want to visit Nanny.'

She opened up the communication flap.

"Do you know Myrtle Cottage in Southwell Lane?"

"Aye," came the gruff reply.

"Take me there, please," she said, thinking how odd Morton sounded.

'Perhaps he has been smoking or has been affected by the wood shavings,' she thought as her nose was itching from inhaling the dust.

The carriage pulled out of the yard and Robina sank back into the seat.

'Morton is taking a strange route,' she wondered, as the carriage hurtled out of the High Street and towards the woods. 'Perhaps he knows a short cut.'

Nanny's cottage was on the outskirts of the village and set back from the road, but she was sure that they were travelling in the opposite direction.

'We should be there by now,' she thought, slightly worried that Morton had lost his way.

She opened the flap to speak to Morton, but, as she did so, she found that something had been jammed into it so that she could not talk through it.

'What is going on?' she worried, as panic began to flood her body.

The carriage was picking up speed and, as she tried the handle to the carriage door, she found it was locked.

"Morton! Morton!" she shouted out, as they rattled down the lanes. "*Please stop*! You are frightening me!"

But Morton took no notice.

'I am being kidnapped!' she said to herself finally, as the awful reality of her situation dawned upon her. 'But why is Morton doing this?'

Fear clutched at her heart as the carriage plunged onwards.

'I could open the window and try to jump out,' she thought, as she held on to the sides of the carriage in order to steady herself, 'but we are going so fast I would surely be killed!'

Tears began to pour down her face as she became more and more terrified.

'Who would want to do such a thing to me?' she asked herself. 'There is only one person I can think of who would dream up such a scheme. But who has she engaged to do her dirty work for her?'

After what seemed like ages, Robina saw that they had come to a halt outside a deserted-looking farm that lay at the end of a long track.

It was so isolated, that in all the years she had lived in the County, she had never come across it.

There was a small yard to one side and the remains of a vegetable patch on the other. There was a barn that was large enough to hold the carriage and a stable for the horses.

Presently the carriage door was wrenched open and a figure lunged inside and pulled her out.

His strong arms grabbed her around the waist and hoisted her down to the ground.

"Put me down, whoever you are!" she cried.

The hollow laughter that answered her told her that it was not Morton who held her fast – no – it was someone else altogether more familiar.

It was *Ellis*.

"What do you want of me and where is Morton?" she howled.

Ellis did not answer, he simply dragged her towards the house.

Bolting the door behind him with his left hand, he threw Robina across the room with the other.

Pulling off the big coachman's coat, Ellis revealed himself for the first time.

"Morton should just about be waking up now. It is a pity he had to suffer – I have no quarrel with him."

"And you have one with *me*?" screamed Robina.

Ellis laughed again – a cruel sneer playing around his features.

"Not really, but you are the means to an end. If my brother sees fit to throw me out and abandon me, then what am I to do for money?"

"So you have kidnapped me in the hope of gaining a ransom? You are very mistaken. My Papa is in London on business and he is not a man who is easily duped into parting with money."

"You silly girl!" snarled Ellis. "You flatter yourself to think that you are worth that much to me!"

"The Earl will miss me and will send a search party for me – you will be discovered and then you will be in dreadful trouble," Robina shouted at him, starting to cry.

"You should save the tears for someone who gives a tinker's cuss," said Ellis coldly, "and as for my brother – what makes you think that he will know where to find you? This house may be on his land, but it could be on another planet for all he knows."

"But Morton – "

"If the silly old fool is awake by now, what will he have to tell? That someone hit him over the head and stole the carriage? He will not have seen me make off with you as I made certain he was out cold before you even left the carpenter's workshop."

Robina lay on the floor, her dress had been torn in the struggle and where Ellis had gripped her so hard, she had bruises in the shape of finger marks.

"In any case, if my brother is too mean to give me money, then there are several others who will for services rendered, so to speak. Your dear stepmother for instance!"

Robina looked up at him in horror.

"You – you know my stepmother?"

Ellis laughed out loudly and regarded her as if she was a small child.

"Of course, I do. You could readily say that Laura and I are on very good terms. She is a most fascinating woman. Although my tastes usually run to much younger types, there is something about her cruelty and ambition that I can understand."

"But you said she paid you money? Why would she do that?"

"To kidnap you, dear simple little Robina! Lord Drury is a very old friend of hers and she wishes to oblige him. I have to say, he must want you very much as the money I was given to abduct you was considerable. Had I known you would command such a very high price, then I would have cut out the middle man and done it myself."

"You mean, I am being bought and sold like a prize heifer?"

"Oh, do not be so harsh on yourself. I like to think of you as being more of a very rare and beautiful fawn!"

The full awful truth was dawning upon her.

So her very real suspicions that her stepmother was not quite what she seemed were proving correct!

'Poor Papa! He is heading for more heartbreak!' she thought, as Ellis moved round the room, testing that all the locks on the doors and windows were fast.

"So, will you send my Papa a ransom note – is that your plan?" she enquired, rubbing her bruises which were beginning to throb.

"Nothing of the sort. Although I must say you have given me an idea."

He paused as if in deep thought and reconsidered,

"But no, I will stick to the original plan as it will have a far greater effect than me holding out for more."

"What do you intend – to do with me – Ellis?"

Robina's voice was quivering as she had seen only too clearly in the past how cruel Ellis could be.

"Oh, I don't intend to do anything other than keep you here until morning. And then, an amenable Vicar will arrive, along with Lord Drury and Laura and you will have no choice in the matter of your marriage – as the Vicar will make certain that you and Lord Drury are joined together right here!

"I had planned to snatch you on your way back to Trentham House, but your outing in my brother's carriage provided the perfect opportunity. It also saved me having to steal the buggy that the estate workers use and provided me with the perfect disguise."

"You cannot do this! You cannot!" cried Robina, as the full horror of what was about to happen to her sank in.

"And, of course, the most delicious bonus to all this is the ridiculous infatuation that my brother seems to have conceived for you. Not only will I be earning for myself a substantial sum of money, but I will be able to pay back that stupid brother of mine in a manner that I could not have dreamed of! I hear the fool has proposed to you – "

'How could he know all about it?' thought Robina, 'Stepmama must have said something to him. And I did not think that she believed me when I told her!'

He stared at her, his black eyes full of contempt.

Robina doubted that Ellis could ever love anyone as much as he loved himself. She hung her head in misery – unable to meet his gaze.

"So, it's true? Hahahaha!"

He threw his head back and laughed loudly.

It was a horrible cold sound that chilled Robina to the core. She wondered what could have happened to him to make him so bitter and twisted.

'Could two brothers ever be so unalike?'

Ellis left her for a moment and Robina could hear him rummaging around next door.

He reappeared shortly holding a length of cord in his hand.

"*No*! Not that, please," pleaded Robina, who feared that in spite of what he had just told her, perhaps he was about to strangle her.

"Don't make a fuss, Robina, my dear," he snarled, coming close to her.

He pulled her to her feet and then threw her into a wooden chair near the fireplace.

Deftly he bound her hands behind her and looped the cord around the back of the chair so that she could not move.

He then took another length of cord from his pocket and wound it round both her ankles several times, before winding it tightly in between so that she could not move her feet.

"There!" he announced, triumphantly. "That should prevent you from running away in the middle of the night like you did the last time.

"Oh, yes – your stepmother has told me everything! I must say, you are far braver than I would have believed – slipping out when everyone was fast asleep and then taking sanctuary at the castle. My word, my brother is a weakling when it comes to a pretty face. He cannot call himself a man!"

Robina was shaking with fear, but it did not prevent her from shouting at Ellis,

"Your brother is a true gentleman. He would never dream of hurting a woman in the way you enjoy and for money too. Ellis, are you not concerned at the shame your actions will bring upon your good family name?"

"What has my family ever done for me?" he grated. "I am to be ostracised and made to pay for one or two little indiscretions. I am certain that my darling brother did not think twice when he raised his sword in India."

By this time Robina was silently crying. She could not bear to hear the Earl spoken of in this manner.

"Your brother is a kind decent and brave man," she cried from deep in her heart. "He is noble and upstanding and would die rather than see his family name besmirched by scandal!"

Ellis looked at her and narrowed his eyes.

"It sounds to me as if he is not the only one who is in love!"

Robina was taken aback – could what Ellis had just said be true?

Was she in love with the Earl and had not realised it?

"No matter, it is of no consequence to me if you are. I am only concerned with receiving the balance of my payment and hurting Robert. I do hope you are going to be very happy with Lord Drury – I hear he is a lusty man for his age – "

Ellis laughed again and got up to leave.

"Now I am feeling hungry and I am meeting Laura at *The Three Oaks Inn*. She is taking full advantage of her husband's absence – believe me!"

Robina watched him put on his cloak and undo the bolts on the cottage door.

"I would say not to wander far, but seeing you tied up so tightly, I do not think you will be going anywhere!" said Ellis with an ugly smirk on his face.

He quickly left and Robina heard a key turning in the lock.

Miserably she stared into empty space and wept.

'So I am to be married to Lord Drury by force,' she sobbed, 'and Stepmama was in league with not only him, but Ellis Hampton as well. Truly, I have been but a pawn in this whole sorry affair!'

*

Meanwhile back at Hampton Castle, the Earl was becoming increasingly concerned.

It was now past three o'clock and there was still no sign of Robina.

'Surely she cannot have been detained for so long with the carpenter?' he pondered, as he sent away his food untouched. 'She had said she may be some time and not wait for luncheon, but this is ridiculous.'

He rose from his desk and paced the room.

'Perhaps she has gone to visit a friend?' he said to himself, 'or she has met with some trouble along the way?'

He rang for Marriott who appeared in a flash.

"Yes, my Lord."

"Marriott, the carriage Miss Melville took out this morning, do you know if it had been checked before they left?"

"I would assume so, my Lord."

"Did the stables ensure that it was in full working order?"

"Of course, my Lord. It has only just been returned from the carriage-works in town. If you recall, there was a loose spoke on one of the wheels which had been causing concern."

The Earl remained silent as he thought.

Finally, he explained.

"It is Miss Melville – she has not returned from the carpenter's workshop. I am concerned that she may have met with an unfortunate accident. I think it would be wise to send someone to the village to make enquiries."

"Very good, my Lord. I will see to it at once."

Marriott disappeared and the Earl began to pace up and down the floor of the study again.

"If anything has happened to her, I will hold myself responsible," he said out loud. "*I love her*! I love her and I will die if she has come to any harm!"

He contemplated saddling up his horse and racing off to find her, but he realised that she might well be found and return to the castle whilst he was out.

'I will stay here at least until the boy we have sent returns,' he resolved.

*

Robina was getting increasingly hungry and thirsty as the hours went by.

There was no sign of Ellis and she felt frightened and alone.

Everything he had told her was going around and around in her head.

Could her stepmother really have taken Ellis as her lover?

And what was it that she stood to gain by forcing her into marriage? If she was left alone with her father, she would be unable to continue her illicit trysts with Ellis.

'I just do not understand what is going on,' sobbed Robina. 'Oh, Mama. If you can see me and hear me, find a way to bring the Earl to me. I cannot remain here and be married off to Lord Drury tomorrow – *I simply cannot*!"

The only one who could save her now was the Earl.

'Oh, Robert,' she whispered, 'I think I have been a fool as far as you are concerned. Please send out a search party for me. I am in very grave peril!'

She prayed and prayed as hard as she could with tears running down her face.

'Do not hesitate – come and rescue me,' she cried, hoping against hope that her prayers would be answered before it was too late.

'Robert, oh, Robert – '

CHAPTER TEN

While Robina was trying to prevent her limbs from going to sleep, being so tightly tied to the chair at the farm, the Earl was beside himself with worry at the castle.

He continued to pace up and down the study until the stable boy returned a few hours later.

"Where is Miss Melville?" he called, as he ran out to the drive to meet him.

"Couldn't find 'er, my Lord," panted the stable boy. "I went to Mr. Armstrong's workshop and 'e told me that she 'ad been there earlier for a time and 'ad got back into 'er carriage and left just before lunch."

"But that was hours ago! Has there been no sign of the carriage?"

"No, my Lord."

The Earl dismissed the boy and walked slowly back towards the house. If Robina was not in the village, then, where on earth was she?

'I don't care what has happened to my carriage, my only concern is for her,' he muttered to himself, as he went into the drawing room.

The windows overlooked the drive and gave him a good vantage point should the carriage return.

The drawing room was one of the rooms Robina was helping him to renovate. Although there was nothing structural to change, the Earl had decided that he wanted a different colour scheme and new furnishings.

He picked up a book intending to read it, but found he could not concentrate.

All he could see was Robina's lovely face and the ugly thought that she might be lying somewhere, injured or worse, tore him in two.

He could not rest – he put the book down and went to look out of the windows for a second time.

Straining his eyes he could make out in the distance what appeared to be a cart ambling down the drive.

A shout out in the hall prompted him to leave the window and run outside.

"My Lord!"

The Earl hurried towards the cart, not caring if he appeared undignified in doing so.

As he approached, he could see that two of the villagers were driving it and there was a slumped figure in the back.

'Robina!' he breathed, straining to make out who it was.

But as he drew nearer, he could see that the person in the back of the cart was a man and not Robina.

The cart pulled up to a halt and one of the villagers doffed his cap at the Earl.

"Beggin' your pardon, my Lord, but we found this poor man crawling down the High Street in a daze. He's been hit over the head, so he has."

The Earl leaned over the side of the cart and saw that it was Morton, his coachman, who lay there.

He was semi-conscious and was holding his head and groaning. Congealed blood was caked upon his temple and his hair was matted with the stuff.

"Morton, what has happened to Miss Melville and tell me how you came to be in this terrible state."

"I am so sorry, my Lord, but someone came at me from behind. I was minding my own business at the back of the carpenter's shop, waiting for Miss Melville to come out, when someone hit me over the head."

"I repeat, where is Miss Melville!" he cried again, becoming quite agitated.

"I don't know, my Lord. Whoever knocked me out stole the coach and I suppose Miss Melville with it."

"Abducted! But why? *Why*? Who on earth could have done this to her?"

"I don't know, my Lord. Tis all very curious."

"Take Morton in and see to him at once," ordered the Earl. "He has been a very brave man."

He indicated to the men to take their cart round to the stables and swiftly ran back inside the castle.

"Marriott, I am going out to look for Miss Melville. I would like you to assemble as many of the male servants as you can spare. Tell them to meet me at the stables."

Marriott nodded and hurried away.

The Earl picked up his riding whip and gloves and headed off towards the stables.

The castle became alive with the sound of shouting and people running hither and thither as he strode across the courtyard to where Saladin, his new Arab stallion, was waiting for him.

A small collection of stable boys and grooms were already mounted and ready to obey his commands.

"Come, my fine beast, we shall see if you are as swift as I have been led to believe," whispered the Earl, as he leapt on to Saladin.

As he led the throng down the drive, he murmured under his breath,

'Hold on, Robina, my darling – wherever you are! I am coming for you! Oh, God, I do hope I am in time to rescue you from whatever peril you face.'

*

The afternoon was wearing on into the evening and Robina, still tied to the chair and alone in the cottage at the farm, was becoming more and more distressed.

She had cried and cried until she had no more tears left, and now, she was utterly exhausted.

Every sound she heard outside made her jump and at any moment she expected a drunken Ellis to come crashing in through the door.

'If his idea of a game is to attempt to kiss me in order to frighten me, I cannot bear to think what he might do if he has been drinking at the inn,' worried Robina, as she steeled herself.

'Oh, Mama,' she implored, looking up to Heaven, 'Ask the Earl to make haste to save me! Should Ellis tire of Stepmama's company, he may come back here, seeking mischief!'

Outside the wind was blowing a farm gate open and shut.

Each bang made Robina's heart race so fast that she found it difficult to breathe.

'Oh, Mama. Keep me safe,' she prayed, as the gate banged noisily in the breeze outside.

*

The search party arrived in the village and the Earl wasted no time in locating the carpenter's workshop.

He found it closed, but, undeterred, he hammered on the door until Mr. Armstrong came to answer it.

"My Lord, what a delightful surprise," he declared, wiping cake crumbs from his face.

138

The Earl had obviously interrupted his tea.

"No time for pleasant chit-chat," remarked the Earl, walking into the workshop, much to the amazement of the two workers seated at the bench drinking tea.

"My Lord," they chorused as they jumped to their feet.

"I am looking for Miss Melville. I believe that she was abducted outside your workshop this lunchtime. Did you, by any chance, hear or see anything?"

The men shook their heads and remained standing.

"Sorry, my Lord," said Mr. Armstrong. "I have not seen her since she was here this morning, when she took away a sample of oak panelling to show you."

"She never reached the castle," responded the Earl, "you are all certain that you did not hear or see anything? My coachman, Morton, was clubbed over the head and is now nursing quite a severe wound."

"Goodness," exclaimed Mr. Armstrong. "But it is possible that we wouldn't have heard a thing with the noise of the machinery in here. If we had the saw running even gunpowder going off would not have disturbed us!"

"Thank you, anyway," sighed the Earl, "and I am sorry to have interrupted your tea. Good afternoon."

Mr. Armstrong took him to the rear of the building so that he could view where Robina had last been seen.

He walked over towards the smithy to talk to the blacksmith, but he had not seen anything, as he had been to the ironworks that morning to buy some materials.

Grim-faced the Earl returned to the post where his horse was tethered.

'I will now find Robina, *no* matter what it takes,' he vowed to himself, as he climbed back on to Saladin.

"Where to now, my Lord?" asked one of his men.

"We should split up into groups," he said, taking charge of the situation.

He had faced many dangers in India and mounting a manhunt had been quite commonplace for him.

But never in his life had a search mattered so much to him.

'If anything has happened to Robina, I will never be able to forgive myself,' he repeated over and over as his men formed groups and went riding off in search of her.

*

At *The Three Oaks Inn* in the village, Laura and Ellis Hampton were emerging from their private room.

They both held a look of the truly triumphant.

"His Lordship will be delighted with the way that you have conducted this affair," Laura smirked, diving into the small handbag that swung from her wrist. "Here is the next instalment of your fee – Lord Drury will pay you the remainder tomorrow morning once the ceremony has been conducted."

Ellis fingered the large notes lovingly.

He planted a tender kiss on the bundle, as he gazed lasciviously into Laura's eyes.

"It's been a great pleasure doing business with you. I cannot think why I didn't come to you the moment my brother cut the purse strings!"

"It is of no consequence, Ellis, the important thing is that we have succeeded. Although I would have made certain I achieved my aim in the end, your intervention has brought matters to a much swifter conclusion than I had thought possible. She is safely locked up at the farm, you say?"

"Tied up like a suckling pig, ready for the spit!"

"You have not harmed her too much, I hope, or laid

a finger upon her? His Lordship will not want to receive spoiled goods – "

Ellis caressed the side of Laura's face with his big square hand and let out a low chuckle.

"Fear not – her virtue has not been compromised. Although I must confess, she is a pretty little thing."

"Just curb your impulses, Ellis," she snarled. "Lord Drury is paying you well for your trouble."

"I didn't know that he was an acquaintance of yours before now. Of course I have come across him in London at the *Gaiety Theatre*."

"He and I are distantly related. When I married Sir Herbert, there were certain aspects to my past I wished to remain private – a certain filthy newspaperman found out a titbit or two and attempted to blackmail me on the eve of my wedding. Thank Heavens Lord Drury is a powerfully persuasive man."

"With very deep pockets – " added Ellis.

Laura simply laughed and did not commit herself to a response.

"Ellis, I will see you tomorrow morning. You will, naturally, be a witness?"

"*Naturally*. I am looking forward to it."

He moved towards Laura and planted a kiss on her cheek.

"Now I intend to have a few more drinks to keep out the cold before I return to that dreadful farm."

"Have you fed the girl?"

"No, should I?"

"We will both be in severe trouble if she tells Lord Drury that we mistreated her. I am concerned enough as it is that you have been forced to restrain her in the manner you described – you must take some food and drink back with you."

Ellis curled his lip and ran his fingers through his hair in a dismissive gesture.

"Very well, if you insist. I am certain the landlord will provide me with some bread and cheese."

"Until the morning, then, Ellis," murmured Laura, casting him a sideways glance.

Before she left the inn, she drew a long veil over her features and wrapped her thin cloak around her.

The brougham was waiting outside for her together with the faithful coachman she had brought from London when she married Sir Herbert.

As he took up the reins, she cast one last look up at the window where she had had her tryst with Ellis.

'Nothing can stop me now!' she smiled to herself, with a satisfied air, '*nothing*!'

With one slap of the reins from the coachman, the brougham took off up the road towards an empty Trentham House with Laura ensconced inside, congratulating herself upon her own cunning and resourcefulness.

*

Only a few miles away, Robina was still waiting for Ellis to return. Out of the dirty window, she could see the sun dipping in the sky.

'It will be getting dark soon,' she sighed.

Her thoughts returned to the Earl.

'Was it true what Ellis said?' she ruminated. 'He said it sounded as if I was in love with the Earl! I have had such little experience in the ways of the world – I always believed that I would know when I was in love, yet, I have feelings for him that I cannot explain.'

She sat there solemnly watching the sun go down and examining her heart.

'If I had accepted his proposal when he first offered it, then I would not be in this terrible situation,' she cried to herself, as a chill draught blew under the door. 'Why was I so stubborn?'

She was still tearfully berating herself when Ellis burst in through the door, a bundle in one hand and a bottle of beer in the other.

*

The Earl was becoming increasingly desperate.

He could see that the light was failing and that still, they were no nearer to finding Robina.

"Lighted torches!" he suddenly exclaimed, as they circled the village for the fifth time. "We must find some torches."

They all regrouped and headed off for the smithy where the blacksmith kept his fires burning constantly.

The Earl found him busy shoeing an old carthorse, but he stopped work and brought them some torches.

"Not found 'er yet, then?" he asked soberly, as the men passed around the lit torches.

"No. We have searched every last barn and copse within a five-mile radius."

"You have been to the woods above your castle?"

"That was one of the first places we looked and I am fast running out of places to try."

"Well, good luck, my Lord. Send word when you find 'er."

The Earl turned Saladin onto the road and rode on ahead of his men.

As he approached the next crossroads, he noticed a

stooped figure making her way slowly along the road.

In the twilight he thought he recognised something about the old woman's face.

"I say," he called, making Saladin trot alongside.

The old woman looked up and in an instant, he saw it was who he suspected.

"Nanny!" he shouted. "I am so pleased to see you. Miss Melville has been kidnapped!"

"Oh, oh!" cried Nanny, throwing her hands up to her face. "This is terrible! What happened?"

"All I know is that she was abducted in my carriage this afternoon. She was paying a visit to Mr. Armstong's workshop when it happened."

"This afternoon you say?" queried Nanny, stopping in her tracks. "And she was in your carriage?"

"Yes! Yes!" he answered leaning down to her.

"Oh, goodness. I saw the carriage earlier today and thought it was you in a fine hurry. It was driving like the devil was on its tail and it almost ran me over! I saw it go rushing up the lane by the thatched barn."

"But that leads to a dead end," exclaimed the Earl, quite clearly puzzled.

Nanny laughed and shook her head.

"Ah, I can see you don't know about old Hatcher's farm, then – and it's on your own land as well."

"Hatcher's farm?" he queried, looking blankly at her in the flickering light of his torch.

"Yes, my Lord. The old farm has been empty since the old man died about ten years ago. Go right up the lane and then you come to a track. It's just wide enough to get a carriage through, if I come to think of it. Follow the track for a mile and then it twists through a small copse. Beyond that is the farm."

"Nanny, I could kiss you! Bless you! Bless you!"

"You go and save my Robina, my Lord. I miss her so much since they dismissed me from the house."

"Dismissed? Robina did not say – Nanny, I cannot linger any longer – I must go and find Robina. I will return tomorrow and see if we cannot find you some employment at the castle, if you should wish. As you know, Robina has been working with me there."

"Thank you very much, my Lord. Good luck! God speed!"

The news spread quickly that the search party was heading off towards the crossroads and then up the nearby lane.

The Earl gathered everyone together and addressed them.

"Listen carefully, men. The element of surprise is all-important here. I now strongly suspect that Miss Robina is being held against her will at old Hatcher's farm."

A murmur rose from the group – they shook their heads and looked puzzled.

"I confess that I, too, did not know of its existence up until now, but it is there at the end of the lane. We must be very quiet and you should look to me for instructions once we get there. Is that clear?"

"Yes, my Lord," they chorused.

The Earl raised his torch high above Saladin's head and spurred him into action.

They headed off towards the crossroads and then fell into single file as they trotted up the lane.

As the lane gave way to the track, the Earl had his men extinguish their torches.

"We must not be seen from the house," he warned. "You will follow me."

They set off again and followed the track. The Earl could see both hoof prints and wheel marks in the dusty road.

The men wound their way through the copse and as they rounded the bend, they saw in the distance a light at a window.

"It's the farm," said one.

"Right, five of you come with me. Two of us will kick the door in and the rest must stay close by in case we need reinforcements. Does anyone have a gun on them?"

Two men nodded and patted their saddlebags.

"Good. Only fire if you hear my command or if you hear shots coming from inside. Is that clear?"

"Yes, my Lord."

Taking a deep breath, the Earl jumped down off his horse and was soon joined by a big burly groom.

Together they ran at the door and kicked at it with all of their might.

The door came flying off its hinges and the Earl rushed inside.

The first thing he saw was Robina, tied to the chair, her cheeks stained with tears.

"*Darling*!" he cried, taking a knife out of his pocket and cutting her bonds.

"Robert!" she sighed, fainting into his strong arms as the ropes fell from her.

"Who did this to you?"

Robina was crying so much she could not speak.

She clung on to the Earl as if her life depended on it with her slender arms entwined around his neck.

"Your own brother," she sobbed.

"*Ellis*!" he screamed, horrified, "where is he?"

"I think he has returned to the inn – he came back for a while and gave me some food and then said he had to go out again."

"The inn?"

"Oh, Robert, he is in league with my Stepmama! She had him kidnap me so that she could force me to marry Lord Drury. A Vicar is arriving first thing in the morning to marry us!"

"My brother is as spiteful as he is dissolute. Are there no depths to which he will sink in order to satiate his filthy appetites? He has not – "

"No, Robert, he did not lay a finger on me. I would say that he was under strict orders not to spoil me for Lord Drury."

Robina found herself reddening furiously under her caked tears.

The Earl gently helped Robina up.

Through the window, he could see that his men had brought the carriage out from the barn and had tethered the remaining horse to it along with one of theirs.

'Ellis must have taken the second horse to the inn,' murmured the Earl to himself.

"You and you, go now to the Police and have them arrest my brother Ellis. I do not think he will be difficult to apprehend – he is probably completely drunk by now!"

"You would have your very own brother arrested?" whispered Robina, as he returned to her side.

He gently stroked her hair and her face, gazing at her with such love in his eyes that it made her heart swell.

"He has abducted the woman I love – nothing is a good enough punishment."

"Can you forgive me for being so stupid?" asked Robina.

"Why do you say that?" asked the Earl.

"Because I refused when you asked me to marry you. Oh, Robert, I have only just realised how much I love you. There, I have said it! *I love you*, I love you!"

He was laughing as he kissed her hair, her eyelids and then her lips.

"So, my darling, you have changed your mind and will marry me?" he sighed, as they parted.

Robina looked up at him and smiled,

"Yes, my dearest Robert, I *will*!"

"Then you have made me the happiest man alive!"

They kissed again and again and Robina poured her whole heart and soul into their embrace.

'Truly I have now found Heaven,' she decided, as they nestled close.

Just then, there came a knock on the front door – it was the groom who had helped the Earl kick the lock off.

He had tactfully withdrawn once he had seen how intimate Robina and the Earl were becoming.

"My Lord, beggin' your pardon, but shall we make the carriage ready to take Miss Melville back home?"

"Your father is still away?" asked the Earl.

"As far as I am aware."

"Then please take Miss Melville back to the castle," instructed the Earl, "I have another call to make before this night is over."

He picked up Robina and tenderly carried her out to the carriage, placed her inside and kissed her once more.

"I shall not be long, my darling."

"Where are you going?"

"I wish to speak to Lady Melville."

"Please be very careful," urged Robina, pleadingly,

as she clutched at his jacket lapels. "Stepmama is a force to be reckoned with!"

"Have no fear, Robina. I will return to the castle as soon as I can. My men will make certain that Mrs. Osidge takes good care of you."

With a sign from him the carriage pulled off back down the narrow track.

'And now,' the Earl grunted to himself, as his men dispersed, 'I have an appointment at Trentham House.'

*

As soon as Robina arrived at the castle, she was quickly surrounded by people anxious for her well-being.

Mrs. Osidge made a great fuss of her and took her immediately to the blue bedroom.

She brought her an excellent hot meal followed by a glass of hot milk laced with brandy.

"Drink this now, it will help you sleep," said Mrs. Osidge, shooing away the other servants.

"I don't think I could close my eyes for a second," answered Robina, full of love for the Earl. "I am far too excited."

Mrs. Osidge gave her a knowing smile, one woman to another.

"We will wake you up when his Lordship returns home – have no fear."

With a smile she sank back into the plump pillows and was soon fast asleep.

*

It seemed she had only been dreaming for a short while when Mrs. Osidge was once again standing over her and calling her name.

"Miss Melville! Miss Melville!"

Sleepily Robina rubbed her eyes and yawned.

"Robert – has he returned?"

"Yes," replied Mrs. Osidge with a broad smile, "his Lordship has just arrived home. He is seeing to his horses and should be here very shortly."

Robina climbed out of bed and ran to the mirror on the dressing table.

Her cheeks were flushed pink from her sleep and her hair was coming undone from the pins that had held it.

She poured some water from the jug into the small china ewer on the nearby washstand and splashed her face.

She was just feeling for the towel so that she could dry herself when she sensed that someone was in the room.

"Mrs. Osidge, would you be so kind as to hand me a towel please?" she called.

A towel was placed into her outstretched hand and she brought it up to her face at once.

As she wiped the water from her eyes, she looked up to see that it was not Mrs. Osidge who had handed her the towel, but her own dear Papa!

"Papa!" she cried out, throwing her arms around his neck and kissing his cheek.

"My dearest daughter," he said with emotion in his voice. "Can you forgive me for being such a fool?"

"Papa, what is there to forgive?"

He took her hands and led her to the sofa.

They sat down and she could see that he had tears in his eyes.

"Robina, I have treated you terribly. You did not deserve to be pushed away and ignored in the way I did. I was consumed with grief and then, I came under the thrall of my new wife. I should never have permitted her to so intoxicate me. Please say you will forgive me."

By this time, Robina, too, was in tears.

She saw the way her father was pleading with her and her heart melted all over again.

"Papa," she murmured, taking his hand, "let us put this whole sorry episode behind us and start anew."

"I would like that," answered her father, "and your stepmother shall not trouble you again for a while. I have sent her off on a very long tour of Europe and told her that, whilst she away abroad, she is to reconsider her behaviour towards you and if she does not see fit to change her ways, then I will have no qualms in sending her packing. And, as for this business with Lord Drury, there will be no further talk of marriage to him."

"You would do – this for me?" stammered Robina, shocked and delighted at the same time.

"You are my own flesh and blood and your Mama would be horrified at how I have forgotten that fact, this past year. But no more as I am a changed man."

They embraced once more and Robina noticed that the Earl had quietly entered the room.

He was smiling broadly at the happy scene in front of him.

"And I have more news for you," he said, as the two of them turned to face him.

"This very night Ellis has been arrested and will be charged by the Police with abduction and seeking to extort money through menaces."

"And Stepmama?"

"Your father has decided not to press any charges against her. It would not reflect very well on his reputation if her name – and his – are dragged through the courts."

Robina looked at her father and realised that he had not been informed of the exact relationship between Laura and Ellis Hampton – a discreet veil had been drawn over that particular part of the proceedings.

"And now, Sir Herbert, I have one last matter that requires your attention."

The Earl walked over to Robina and took her by the hand.

Smiling down at her, he began,

"Robina and I have grown very close to each other and our relationship has blossomed into more than that of employer and employee. I have asked her to marry me and she has accepted and, with your permission, we would like to be married as soon as possible."

Sir Herbert jumped up and shook the Earl's hand warmly.

"My dear fellow, I cannot think of anything more wonderful. With you as her husband, I should know that she would be well cared for and cherished.

"And now it is time I took my dear daughter back home. We have so much to discuss, although I am certain that she will be returning to the castle to resume her duties as soon as she has recovered from her terrible ordeal."

"I will ask for your carriage to be brought round to the front of the castle," said the Earl, "and you may take her home at once."

"Now if you will excuse me," replied Sir Herbert, "I will make arrangements for my horse to be brought back to Trentham House in the morning."

With one last smile for Robina, her father rose and tactfully withdrew.

As the door closed behind him, the Earl sank down on the sofa and pulled Robina into his arms.

"My dearest love," he sighed, as he kissed her tenderly, "the day that I rode into your stables at Trentham

House was the most fortunate day of my life. If I had not done so, I might not have found you.

"And now, I am to be married to the most beautiful girl in the world and I have never been happier in all my life."

Robina laid her head on his chest.

"I believe that Mama has been looking down from Heaven and smiling on us. Not so long ago, I was very lonely and confused. My Papa did not seem to want me and even Nanny was sent away, but now I have a whole new life in front of me. Please, dearest, might we find a place for Nanny at the castle?"

The Earl laughed and stroked her cheek.

"I have already spoken with your Nanny on that very subject. It was Nanny who led me to you as she was nearly run over by my carriage when Ellis was driving it to the farm after he had abducted you.

"I came across her while I was searching for you this evening and she told me she had been dismissed. Of course, we shall have her with us at the castle, forever and ever, should you wish it."

"And when we have our own children, Nanny can help me look after them," suggested Robina, so contented and at peace with the whole world that she did not wish the moment to end.

"To think that I have now found you again after so many years of searching and it was the Tower itself that brought us together."

"It was my Mama up in Heaven," replied Robina, her eyes cast skywards. "She is never far from me and I know that it was she who led us to each other."

"Darling, I shall love you forever and all Eternity – you need never doubt it."

"And I will love you and adore you forever too," answered Robina, her heart soaring to meet his and their souls entwining. "In this life and all the lives we still have to live."

"Forever and beyond," he murmured, as they sank into a warm and everlasting kiss of love.